JAKE HALBERT, Woods Cross High School's football coach, is dying of cancer. A hero to everyone but his seventeen-year-old son, Jim, he is still out there on the field yelling at the players and fighting for time. As Jake's condition worsens, Jim confronts his urgent need to know his father before it's too late. But Jake is not an easy man to know.

Jim tries to keep his feelings private, but his father's dying seems to belong to everyone. Jim's favorite English teacher uses it as he teaches a unit on death. Jim's beautiful girl friend Mimi yells it across the football field in a get-well cheer. His childhood friend and teammate Bud Alden, who loves Jake in a way Jim never could, denies it. And as Jim struggles to understand his own feelings—for the father he thought he hated, for the girl he thought he loved, for the game he played only because it was expected of him, and for the newcomer Gus (a.k.a. Agnes)—everything pulls into a different focus.

With unique perception and a compelling mixture of sadness and humor, Barbara Stretton gives us an all-together real portrait of a father-son relationship, and a life-embracing exploration of love and dying.

You Never Lose

BY BARBARA STRETTON

Alfred A. Knopf · New York

Fic
STR

This is a Borzoi Book
Published by Alfred A. Knopf, Inc.

Copyright © 1982 by Barbara Stretton
All rights reserved under International and Pan-American Copyright Conventions. Published in the United States by Alfred A. Knopf, Inc., New York, and simultaneously in Canada by Random House of Canada Limited, Toronto. Distributed by Random House, Inc., New York. Manufactured in the United States of America

10 9 8 7 6 5 4 3 2 1

Library of Congress Cataloging in Publication Data
Stretton, Barbara. You never lose.
Summary: At the beginning of his senior year, Jim learns that his father, football coach, and hero, whom he so closely resembles, is dying of cancer.
[1. Death—Fiction. 2. Fathers and sons—Fiction. 3. Football—Fiction] I. Title.
PZ7.S91647Yo   [Fic]   81-15557
ISBN 0-394-85230-3   AACR2
ISBN 0-394-95230-8 (lib. bdg.)

TO MY MOTHER

You never lose.
But sometimes the clock
runs out on you.

VINCE LOMBARDI

YOU NEVER LOSE

1

For Mimi, Jim Halbert chose his pale yellow crew-neck to wear on the first day of school. Yellow for Mimi because it matched her hair. And his newest pair of jeans. He knew he'd be noticed in the halls, so he wanted to look his best. Not because kids would look at him, point at him, come up and tell him how sorry they were, but because of Mimi.

By third period, if not before, everyone would know about Jake Halbert—the coach—his father—about his having cancer. What Jim had known for five weeks, what Jim had lived with like a cancer of his own growing silently inside of him, would now be open and ugly. Mimi would know, too, of course, but that would be different. All summer he'd waited for the day he'd see Mimi again, her lovely face with its slim nose, the way she pouted her lips and tossed her long white-blond hair. But more than that, more than her prettiness and her warm lovemaking, he'd waited to talk to her. Mimi would understand what he was going through. He could tell her how he felt about what was happening to him.

They'd quarreled at the beginning of the summer. He told her he didn't see why she had to be a counselor at a camp when her family had plenty of money for college. His housepainting job was different; he needed the money. But she just tossed that white-blond hair and said if he was gone all day painting, then she might as well be doing something too. She wrote to him every week, filling onionskin paper with her schoolgirl rounded script, complaining about the camp. But he didn't answer her letters. At first he was still annoyed and decided to keep her guessing. Then he learned about his father. After that he couldn't write. He could tell her if he saw her, he knew that. He could hold her close and pour out all the pain, but he couldn't face a sheet of blank paper and form words. Not after the night his mother told him.

He'd come home hot and smelling of paint, wanting a shower and a cold Coke. The house was closed up in spite of the heat, and the shades were drawn.

He'd found his mother sitting alone in the dark living room, staring at her folded hands. She'd looked as though she had been sitting there all day.

"Mother?"

"Sit down, Jim."

She'd said a lot that night, he knew. They'd talked

for over an hour, filling the dark air with words. But only four words stayed in his mind: "Your father has cancer."

The house had been so quiet. There was no TV sports blaring from the basement, no throbbing rock music from his sister Liz's room. It was the silence he remembered whenever he thought about that night —the silence and his mother's hands clamped together in her lap.

He was combing his hair in front of the full-length mirror on his bedroom door when the door opened. His image slid away and became a fourteen-year-old girl, his sister, Liz.

Almost as if he were her mirror, she asked, "How do I look?"

Liz had their mother's tight dark curls instead of Jake's wheat-colored hair as Jim did. She was wearing a crisp cotton blouse and jeans. She looked pretty and suddenly grown-up. But he wasn't about to tell her that right off.

He cocked his head to one side and narrowed his eyes. "*Hmmm.*"

"Come on, Jim." She touched her hair. "I shouldn't have had it cut. I look dumb."

"No, Liz, you look good." All summer, what he'd seen of her, she'd been the same little girl she'd always been. But now she was a high school girl, and he realized in that peculiar way time has of shifting, she'd caught up with him. The three years between them was no longer so very much. It gave him an uneasy feeling.

"You sure? I mean, should I put on a sweater or anything? Sue Alden says they're wearing blouses now."

"Well, if Sue Alden says so, it must be so."

"She does know. I mean, she keeps track of those things. They're important, she says."

Jim smiled, remembering the way he'd felt going to Woods Cross as a freshman. After the middle school, it was a shock to find yourself so small and so frightened. Of course, he was known almost instantly by his looks, or rather by his father's looks. It was as if his coming had been expected, prepared for. He laughed ironically. The Second Coming, ha, ha.

"I'm heading for breakfast, kid," he said. "You want a ride this morning?"

"No. Sue and I are taking the bus. You sure I look all right?" She headed toward her room, then turned.

"You look fine."

"Jim?" Her face became serious, the uncertainty changing to fear. "Will they know? The kids? About Dad?"

"I don't know, Liz. Probably. Things get around fast."

She nodded, then opened the door of her own room.

"I wish they didn't have to know," she said quietly, almost to herself.

His mother sat alone at the kitchen table, sipping coffee. She was wearing a neat suit and white blouse. She'd tied a dark string bow at her throat, but it drooped like a frown. He kissed the top of her head and went to the refrigerator. He pulled out the carton of milk and took a long swallow.

"I wish you'd use a glass," she said absently, one of those things she always said but didn't expect him to do.

"Sorry." He took a glass from the cupboard and joined her at the table. He spread a piece of toast with jam and bit into it.

They sat in silence. The house, too, seemed unusually quiet for a school morning. Liz wasn't playing her stereo, and there was no swish of water from the shower. "Dad go in early?"

"Yes." She sighed. "Of course."

"Probably worried about his classes. Or the team."

"Something like that." She put the coffee mug down and pushed her chair away from the table. "I'd better get to work. Is Liz up?"

"Yes. All excited about school."

She turned her back, putting the milk and butter into the refrigerator. Jim noticed how her shoulders were drawn tightly together, her movements jerky with tension.

"Mom?"

"Yes?"

"Should—should Dad have gone back? To school, I mean?"

She spun around, her face distorted with anger. "He didn't have to. He has enough sick leave for most of the year. He didn't have to."

"Then why—" Jim started, but stopped. She had turned back again and grabbed hold of the refrigerator door handle, clutching it as if trying to hold on to something, anything. He started to rise, but then Liz came in.

"Geez, I'm going to miss the bus. High school starts so early. I can't get used to it." She poured a glass of orange juice and drank it quickly, grabbed a piece of toast, and was gone.

"I—I'd better get going too," he mumbled, not looking at his mother.

"Jim?" She turned. Her face was very pale, almost translucent. "Look out for your father today."

"Sure, Mom." He left the room hurriedly before she said more.

As he drove to school he thought about those words. You said, "look out," when you warned someone about a danger. But "look out for your father," she'd said. Of course, she merely meant see that he's all right. But somehow the other meaning of the words—look out, be wary—kept taunting him. Hadn't he always done that—looked out for his father, gotten out of his way? He felt the tension at the back of his neck as if a strong hand were gripping him.

He waved to some of his friends who were lounging against the glass wall of the office. Len Wilson beckoned him over.

"Hey, Jimbo, how's it going?" Len's handsome black face relaxed into an easy smile. Len was small, but under the football letter jacket his muscles were taut as wire. The other boys in the group, most of them players from the team, greeted him.

Jim answered Len. "I'll know better after first period. I have trig."

"Yeah? Who do you have? Bowden?"

"Yep."

The halls were jammed. Girls passed, clutching their notebooks, smiling at the knot of boys by the office. We're the jocks, Jim thought, the football team—cream of Woods Cross manhood. And we'll never have it this good again.

"What's happened to the bell?" one of the boys asked. "It should have rung ten minutes ago."

Jim glanced at his watch.

"No teachers around either," Len commented. "What gives?"

Then the teachers appeared, coming out of the side door of the cafeteria. As they passed the boys, Jim heard one of them say, "God, what a way to start the year." Someone else nodded. The bell rang.

As they went down the hall Len asked, "Set for the season?"

"I guess so, Len. I don't know."

"Missed you at August practice."

"Yeah. Well, I had this job I had to finish up. I told Dad."

Len laid a hand on Jim's shoulder. "He made a few cracks about you. Looks like you'll be in for another tough year."

Jim didn't answer, but pretended to be watching the passing girls. Len didn't know yet; none of the guys did. Jake wouldn't tell them, and he was still as loud and gruff as ever, so no one would even suspect anything was wrong. But they'd know soon enough. The other teachers would find out, and it would get around the school. Jim was sure of it.

"The team ain't much good this year for some reason. I guess we need your power."

"My power? Fat chance. What you need is Gardner and McCullough back."

"Well, we'll just have to send to Purdue or Princeton or wherever, won't we?" Len shrugged. "It'll come together. See you tonight."

Jim watched Len go down the hall. Len was a good guy, he thought, somebody I could maybe talk to. Len was the one who always talked him into staying on the team. Every time Jim swore he'd quit and never set foot on that field again, Len was there to talk him out of it.

Last year, for example, after Jim ran that touchdown in, and Jake had called him a Saturday hero, Len said something to him that really struck home. "He needs you, Jim. And he doesn't like needing anyone. That's why he rides you."

Jim didn't quite believe that, but it sounded good, anyway. He'd often thought of that comment of Len's during the summer, watching his father come home from coaching. If Jake needed him, he had a funny way of showing it.

The thought of practice that afternoon lay like a lump inside Jim's stomach. All he could do was hope for the best. There was no way he could quit the team this year.

On the way to first period he looked for Mimi. But he got to Mr. Bowden's room without catching a glimpse of her.

Mr. Bowden wasn't there yet, so the students were talking, perched on their desks and leaning against the windows. Jim didn't join them, but found a seat near the back and tried to set his mind back into the groove of school.

Mr. Bowden came in, humped forward as if carrying the ball in a scrimmage. "Sit down, you clowns," he shouted. "The bell rang five years ago."

The class settled into place. Mr. Bowden opened a file folder and glanced from it to the faces of the students, taking the roll. He didn't need to call names. He'd had most of them in algebra last year.

He'd stop occasionally to make a remark, call someone a clown, and ask why they were taking trigonometry when they couldn't add two and two—but it was all in fun, and the kids knew it. Then he came to Jim and his face changed. The good-natured smirk disappeared and his eyes softened.

"Halbert," he said gently, "good to have you." The other students, noticing the change, glanced at Jim. No joke? No crack about being a jock? Nothing to make Jim blush? Not even sarcasm? What gives?

By third period everyone knew. A girl in history class turned in her seat and told Jim how sorry she was to hear about his dad. "Our homeroom teacher told us," she said. "The principal told them this morning. I think he's the bravest guy—to come to school and everything. You must be proud."

Jim didn't tell her how he really felt, he just nodded and dropped his gaze to his desk. He wasn't proud, he was ashamed. He wished his father wasn't at school, being brave and noble and all those other things. When his typing teacher had stopped by his desk and laid her large hand, heavy with rings, on his shoulder, it had lain there like a burden.

Going through the halls between classes was even worse. Kids looked at him, then looked away. He felt like a freak.

Suddenly a firm hand encircled his arm and wrenched him out of the crowd. Bud Alden's boyish face was twisted with fury. "You goddamned bastard!" Bud shouted.

It was not their friendly banter, but Jim pretended it was. "Hey, you dumb jock, what d'you mean shoving me around?"

"Damn you, Halbert. Why didn't you tell me?"

"Tell you?"

"About your dad. I have to hear it from a kid in gym class. A kid I don't even know."

"I'm sorry, Bud."

"Sorry? Is that all you can say? That you're sorry?" Bud's anger turned suddenly to grief. "Then it is true. I hoped because you hadn't said anything—hadn't told me yourself—I hoped it wasn't true."

"It's true, Bud."

Bud let go of his arm and turned toward the wall, laying his hand flat against the tiles. "God. Coach. God," he said, choking on his tears.

Jim wanted to comfort his friend, but he didn't know how. He didn't want to pour empty words into the ears of this guy he'd known all his life. He laid his hand on Bud's shoulder for a moment. "Look, old buddy," he said. "I've got to get to class."

Bud turned again. "When—when did you find out?"

"July. He went in for a checkup before school started."

"July? Did you say July? That's only about a month ago."

"Yes." Five weeks, he almost said. Five weeks and two days and—

"Then—then he hasn't had it very long?"

"They don't know. It wasn't there last winter when he had that minor surgery. The hemorrhoid thing."

"But it's there now? I mean—it couldn't be a mistake or anything?"

"No. There's no mistake. Look, Bud—"

"But maybe they caught it soon enough. They can operate."

Jim gazed at his friend. He'd known Bud all his life. They'd been best friends since the day they met on the sidewalk that ran in front of their houses when they were four years old. He felt like a brother to Bud, an older brother somehow, even though they were the same age. He wanted now to lie to Bud, something he'd never done. He wanted to hold out hope with a lie. But he couldn't. "No. It's too late."

"No? But only since July—"

"It's gone too far. There's no chance of operating."

The hall was nearly empty now. Bud's hand slid down Jim's arm, his fingers gripping Jim's, clutching. "You—you should have told me, Jim. I shouldn't have had to hear it this way. You owed me that much."

Bud let go and turned, walking down the hall without looking back. I owe you? Jim thought. It's *my* dad, for Christ's sake.

2

Jim was on his way to study hall when he saw his father heading toward the office. He shuffled like an old man, bent over, his left hand flat against his hip.

Jim had seen him like that once before, but he'd nearly forgotten. One evening during the summer, he had pulled in behind his father's car in the driveway. He caught a glimpse of Jake bent over and shuffling up the walk, but before his mind had registered what it meant, Jake suddenly straightened up.

Just as he had that night, Jake straightened up as he went in the office, the springiness returning to his step.

He's in pain, Jim realized. When he's alone—or thinks he is—he gives in to it. But when anyone is around, he pretends.

Jim hurried to study hall, trying not to think about what he'd seen. He hoped his father hadn't seen him.

Mrs. Linden was marking the roll when he arrived. She frowned and held out her hand for a pass without looking at him.

"I—I have no late pass," he muttered. "I'm just late." He tried to make up an excuse, but he was no good at lying. He didn't know what you did when you came to class late without a pass. He was not to find out that day either.

Mrs. Linden looked up, recognized him, and smiled. She let her hand fall to her side. "Oh, Jim. I'm sorry. How are you?"

It was not just a greeting, but an actual question, one he was expected to answer. His teachers had been asking it all morning, but all he'd come up with so far was the standard, "Fine."

She made no mark in her roll next to his name, but capped her pen and surveyed the room. "I'm afraid there's only the front table left," she said. "Perhaps tomorrow we can find you something less, er, conspicuous."

"This is fine," he said, reddening. What did she mean about being conspicuous? Did she think he wanted to hide in the back somewhere?

As he headed toward the table, he glanced around the room, looking for familiar faces. Then he saw Mimi and his heart leaped.

She was watching him, her arched brows drawn together. She looked so beautiful, her skin tanned, her hair glistening. He cursed himself for not getting to study early enough to sit by her. He smiled at her, but she didn't smile back. He ducked his head and sat down. He opened his trig book and tried to study the problems, but his mind kept tugging back to Mimi. She must be mad at me, he thought, for not writing. But I did call her over the weekend. She just wasn't there. He glanced at his watch, even though he knew they were only five minutes into the period. It would be forty-five minutes before he could talk to her. He wondered how he could wait that long.

Suddenly the door burst open and crashed against the wall. "Is this Caf two?" demanded a tall, thin girl in a loud voice.

Mrs. Linden regarded the girl over the rims of her half-moon glasses. "It is. But it's being used as a study hall this period, I'm afraid. Lunch begins at—"

"Yeah, I know." The girl strode forward. "I'm in this study, they tell me. Crazy place. I never heard of a whole period just for study."

"In that case, young lady, I would appreciate it if you would close the door."

The girl glanced over her shoulder. "Oh, yeah. Sorry." She strode back and slammed the door. The study hall students broke into laughter.

"Will you people settle down, please?"

Jim smiled. The oppression of a few minutes before lifted as if a cool breeze had whipped through the room. He studied the girl. Her lank brown hair was uncombed. In a face that was too thin, her slit of a mouth was turned up slightly at the corners as if she was enjoying the sensation she was creating. Her black eyes were touched with good humor.

"Yeah," she addressed the group. "You guys cut the horseplay. This is a *class* place." That brought more laughter.

"Young lady, I will thank you to keep your voice down."

"You're welcome, ma'm." Then she addressed the group again. "See, a class place. They tell you 'thank you' and 'please' like crazy around here. Back where I come from in West Virginia—"

"Come over here this minute!" Mrs. Linden's voice cut into the confusion like a knife. The girl shrugged her thin shoulders and went over to Mrs. Linden's desk. Mrs. Linden held out her hand.

The girl reached out her own hand and took Mrs. Linden's, giving it a firm shake. "Now, that's what I like about this place. Real friendly. Pleased to meet you. I'm Gus Palmer."

The class broke up again.

Jim liked her. He didn't quite know why, but something in him responded to her brash ways. She looked like she belonged on a Western movie set, leaning against the corral chewing on a blade of straw. And in spite of her unattractiveness, he found he was aroused by her. He shook his head. He'd been away from Mimi much too long, that was all.

He looked at Mimi again. She smiled at him and twirled her finger around her ear, mouthing the word "crazy." He made signs for her to meet him after study. She nodded.

Mrs. Linden had extracted her hand from Gus's firm grip. "I'm asking you for that pass you have in your other hand. I assume it's a late pass."

The girl seemed to discover the wad of yellow paper crumpled in her hand. "Oh, yeah. This." She thrust it forward.

Mrs. Linden took it between her fingers and unfolded it gingerly as if expecting something to crawl out of it.

"That's another thing about this here school," Gus addressed the class. "They give you so many passes. Jesus, at my old school, we used to—"

"I don't seem to have your name on my role, uh—Gus, is it?" Mrs. Linden acted relieved.

The girl leaned over. "Yeah, you do. There it is." She pointed to the list. "Palmer. That's me."

"But that says Agnes Palmer."

"Yeah. But I go by Gus. Wouldn't you?"

"I can't think why. Very well, if you will quietly take a seat. There's room in the front row."

"I always sit in back. That way I can—"

"There isn't any room in back, Agnes."

Gus frowned, then her gaze fell on Jim. "Yeah, well, on second thought, this looks okay." She went over and clapped Jim on the shoulder. "Hiya. Gus Palmer." She stuck her hand out.

He took it and received a wrenching handshake. "Jim. Jim Halbert."

She drew up the chair next to his and tossed her books onto the table.

Up close, Jim realized she was prettier than he'd first thought. She had small features and her skin, though pale, was clear. A row of freckles peppered her nose, which turned up slightly at the tip, giving her an impish look. Still, it was an open, honest face that looked into his, one free of guile.

"Are you new here?" Jim asked.

"Yeah. Man, is this ever some place."

"Where are you from?"

"West Virginia. Little town way near the border, name of Harrington. This school is bigger than my whole town. I've been lost all morning and in trouble since first period. What'd you say your name was?"

"Jim Halbert."

"Halbert?" She riffled through her papers. "Your dad teach gym here?"

"Yes. He—he's Coach Halbert."

"Yeah, that's right. I have him second period. I think. It's all a blur." She leaned back in her chair and crossed one leg over the other. "This is a nice town, though. Real upper class. Of course, I don't live in the fancy section. We got a place over the cheese shop downtown. Ain't bad, though. You see, my dad—"

"Will you please settle down, Agnes?" interjected Mrs. Linden.

"Yeah, yeah. Just getting acquainted." Gus leaned forward and opened her tattered notebook. "She's a bitch on wheels, isn't she?"

Jim smiled, but he didn't answer. Gus shuffled her papers. Jim wondered how her notebook could have gotten in such a sorry state on the first day. On the first half of the first day, in fact.

"You know anything about algebra?" she asked him.

"Yes, a little. I took it last year."

"Well, I ain't never took it. But they tell me I got to have it to graduate. I went there this morning and I don't understand diddlysquat. First day and already I'm three weeks behind." She produced a dog-eared yellow paper. "This is our homework, and I don't even know where to begin."

Suddenly Mrs. Linden loomed over them. "Jim, I'm sorry, but maybe you can make it clear what our rules are here. I don't seem to be able to get across to—uh—Miss Palmer—about not talking during study."

"Holy shit! He's only helping me with my math. You don't have to give him a hard time."

"I wasn't giving him a hard time, Agnes. What I said was meant entirely for you."

"Well, Christ, if you meant me, why did you say 'Jim'? My name ain't Jim. And it ain't Agnes, either."

The class had almost settled down, but her outburst broke them up once more.

Mrs. Linden took a deep breath. "Come with me. And bring your books." She went briskly to her desk and began scribbling on a piece of paper.

"Does she mean me this time?" Gus asked.

"I'm afraid so."

"Shit. I haven't been here ten minutes and already I'm kicked out. I'll never get the hang of this joint." She got up and stuck out her hand again. "Catch you later, Halbert."

She left study hall much as she'd entered it, with a loud crash of the double doors and a note crushed in her hand.

After she'd gone the room seemed empty, as if a vital part of the air had seeped out. Jim glanced back. Everyone was staring at the door. He caught Mimi's smile and returned it, but not with the enthusiasm he'd felt earlier.

Then he noticed the torn yellow paper still lying at Gus's place, the math assignment she'd said she didn't know "diddlysquat" about.

She'd doodled on the margins so that the problems were encased with pictures like an illuminated manuscript. It looked as though she'd spent the whole period sketching her classmates. He recognized some of them, and at the top was an unmistakable portait of Mr. Bowden. She'd even caught the expression of mild distraction in his eyes and the lines etched on his forehead. She may not know diddlysquat about algebra, but she sure could draw. He slipped the paper into his own notebook.

He waited by the door for Mimi. She seemed to take forever, stopping to chat, tossing her hair over her shoulder, laughing. When at last she joined him, her smile was guarded. "Hi." Her tone was cool.

Jim slipped his arm around her. She was wearing a yellow sundress with string straps over the golden tanned shoulders. He felt the silkiness of her shimmering hair on his arm. "God, I missed you," he whispered.

She flipped his arm off her shoulder. "You certainly didn't act like it. I thought you were going to write. I waited and waited, but not a word. I was sure you'd found yourself another girl friend. Every day I kept expecting to get a letter telling me it was all over."

"Nothing like that, Mimi. Believe me."

"I nearly went crazy up there. You have no idea. The kids were terrors. It was like having a hundred little brothers instead of just two. God, it was awful."

"Why didn't you quit?"

"I couldn't. I had a contract and anyway—" She

paused and licked her full lower lip. "Anyway, it had its moments."

He saw something in her eyes and knew she was thinking more than she was saying. "Such as?"

"Well, there was this lake. It was the most gorgeous thing I've ever seen. I'd sneak away from the camp whenever I could—mostly at night when the brats were asleep—and I'd swim there." She giggled. "Sometimes I swam naked. It was warm enough and well, private enough."

"Alone?"

"Of course, alone. What do you think? It was a camp, for Christ's sake, and all the counselors were girls. But it was nice—that part of it anyway."

Jim looked at her, his mind dwelling on the image of Mimi swimming naked in the lake. His body ached for her. He drew her close as they walked, but he felt her stiffen against him.

"I wish you'd written," she said.

"I called. Saturday and again yesterday. Your brother—one of them—took a message. Didn't you get it?"

"No. They never tell me when someone calls. You should have kept trying."

"I did keep trying. I began to think you were avoiding me."

She studied him again, the same expression in her eyes. "I wasn't, Jim, but I wanted to be, well, by myself a bit after I got back. I did get the message, but I didn't, well, I didn't want to see you right away."

"*Oho!* Now who's avoiding who?"

She sighed. "It's awful being back, you know? I still keep thinking about that lake. And then when I got to school and heard everybody talking about your dad, well, I felt so awful. At first I didn't want to see you. I didn't know what I could say to you, or anything. It's all so confusing."

Jim nodded. "Yes. For everyone."

"Look, I've got to get to class," she said. "Meet me at lunch, and we can talk some more, okay? I'll save a table."

She turned, her skirt whirling around her shapely legs, and hurried down the hall. Jim smiled. He'd almost forgotten what she was like, so hard to hold, like quicksilver.

3

Jim settled back in his seat and stretched his long legs across the aisle. For the first time that day he felt calm. This was Dundee's class. Dundee wasn't there yet, but already Jim was looking forward to the class. He looked around.

There was the fish tank beside him, and in the back the old-fashioned refrigerator. And the whiff of formaldehyde. That smell more than anything else took Jim back to his freshman year in this room.

Dundee had started off by apologizing for holding an English class in a science room, but after a while it didn't matter. He knew how to bring a group of students together, to make them one.

He read aloud to them, his voice mellifluous when he read poetry, fierce when he read the ravings of Macbeth, almost a whisper when he captured the yearnings of young Anne Frank. But it wasn't just the class that made it for Jim that year. It was the evenings spent with a select few students at Dundee's apartment knocking around ideas. And that group, Jim realized, was now reassembled in the same science room waiting for the teacher to make his entrance. He caught Len Wilson's eye and they exchanged grins.

Dundee came in, his longish hair flying, his tie askew, a bundle of paperback books under his arm. He kicked the door closed and dropped his load onto the desk. He perched on the edge of it and let his eyes roam over the upturned faces. He ran his fingers through his hair and tucked his tie into his jacket, then smiled and nodded a silent greeting to each student. But when his gaze fell on Jim, his face changed. His eyes deepened and seemed to hold Jim's with a question.

Then he turned away, busying himself with the roll, then looked once more over the class, this time pointedly avoiding Jim. He launched into a nervous little speech about the requirements of AP English, his grading system, spelling, vocabulary and book reports, covering the blackboard with scrawls.

At last, running out of blackboard and breath, he settled once more on the edge of the desk. Jim glanced up from the notes he'd been taking to see Dundee's blue eyes once more studying him, the question still there.

"We're going to do a literature unit that might upset you," Dundee said, and for a moment Jim thought he was speaking directly to him. But Dundee's eyes had moved to the girl across the aisle, then further to the boys at the back.

Jim relaxed. It had been a coincidence that Dundee spoke at exactly the moment he was looking at him.

"But before I tell you about it," he went on, "I want to tell you why. Bear with me if this seems roundabout—I will get there. The story begins in Bermuda."

"Oh, wow!" one of the girls chirped.

"You know Bermuda?"

"Yes. We went there last year. Where did you stay?"

"A small hotel called the Reefs in Southampton. On the south shore. But let me get on with my story, Sandy, and we can share our love of Bermuda later." He turned the corners of his mouth up slightly and let his gaze linger on her just long enough to cause her to blush.

Watching, Jim realized something he hadn't taken in before. Dundee was an actor. He knew how to use his eyes and his voice for effect, to get a response from his audience.

"One morning while walking on the beach, I saw a dead sea gull. It looked as if it had been washed up by the tide. It had been dead a long time, was quite decayed."

"*Yuck*," one of the other girls exclaimed.

"Yes, Rosa, *yuck*. That's just how I felt. I'd been having the most glorious early morning jog along the beach—Horseshoe Bay it's called, and it goes on for miles. I was all alone. My wife was still asleep at the hotel. I'd had an impulse to get up and take the motorbike down the road, and when I saw this lovely expanse of beach, I decided to leave my footprints in the virgin sand."

Some of the girls tittered and the boys made catcalls. What's he getting at, Jim wondered, still aware of how Dundee was playing to his audience rather than just telling a story.

"And then this carcass that had once been a sea gull washed up practically at my feet. Actually, it wasn't a sea gull, but one of those white seabirds they have in Bermuda that they call longtails. That made it worse. The waves washed at it, making its head wag, its wings flap. It looked alive, this grotesque thing that had once been a beautiful bird."

He paused. There was no sound in the room but the ticking of the clock.

"That's really sad, Mr. Dundee," Sandy said, her eyes shining. "I remember those birds."

"What was really sad, Sandy, was the way I felt. This was death—as much a part of life as anything else. And I didn't want to cry, or to rejoice in the bird's existence, in its beauty when it was alive. I wanted to puke."

The class laughed nervously.

"I wanted to throw up at the sight of this—this natural phenomenon. To get away, not look. But I didn't. I stood there. I made myself stand there and look at that bird. And I looked up in the sky at the other birds circling, their long tails making momentary spirals; and a steady calm overtook me. I began to feel better. I began to rejoice that life existed in all its beauty and all its ugliness."

He'd started with a soft voice, but it had risen in a steady crescendo. Now the rich vibrant tones filled the room. "I could not get in touch with my feelings until I let go of all my preconceived notions about death being unnatural, ugly." He stopped and a hush hung in the room. He let his eyes wander over the class once more, pausing here and there to read the expression in the students' eyes. When he reached Jim, his eyelids fluttered and his eyes shifted quickly away.

"That's when I decided. To do this unit." Once more he paused.

Jim was as caught up in the story as the rest of the class, but somehow his mind kept tugging at the thought of what a ham Geoff Dundee was. He was a clever storyteller who knew when to speak and when to remain silent, when to whisper and when to shout, playing his class as a musician plays on his instrument. He began to wonder if it had been Dundee's ideas or his delivery that had captured him.

Dundee's voice was loud once more. "The unit we're going to do is called 'Death, the Final Taboo.'"

Jim was startled. He'd been letting his mind wander and had not been prepared for the announcement. It stuck him like a blow.

Dundee swiveled and picked up one of the books from his desk. He held it up, panning it so the class could see the title: *Death Be Not Proud.*

Jim felt a knot of tension tighten in his stomach.

"We're going to bring death out of the closet," Dundee was saying, getting excited, "or should I say, out of the casket." He lowered his voice once more—*pianissimo*—and the class leaned forward, straining to hear. "I decided all this on a beach in Bermuda looking at a dead bird. Then I came to school and learned that death is much closer than that. Death is here at Woods Cross, and we must deal with that."

Several heads turned to look at Jim, then quickly looked away. The knot in Jim's stomach tightened, and he felt the rising wave of nausea.

So that was it, Jim thought bitterly—the question buried in Dundee's eyes at the beginning of the period. How can I use him? If I want to shock the class, how can I do it best? With a unit on death at the precise time when Jake Halbert, the hero of Woods Cross, was lumbering up the hall in death's shadow.

Dundee had gone to the blackboard and was erasing it with sweeping strokes. Then, with some of the scrawl still on it, he grabbed the chalk and wrote in large block letters, "Death, the Final Taboo," breaking the chalk with a sweep of underlining. He turned to the class, no longer the actor, now the teacher making an assignment. "That's your first vocabulary word—"

"Death?" one of the girls asked.

Dundee paused, then a wry smile crossed his face. "I meant 'taboo,' Linda. But I like your idea better. Yes, much better." He turned back to the blackboard, picked up the fragment of chalk and circled the word "Death."

"Define death. 'What death means to me.' Five hundred words, first draft due tomorrow." As if on cue, the bell rang.

No one spoke to Jim, or even met his eye as he left the room, but when he turned down the hall, he heard his name called. Len came loping up.

"What's with Dundee this year?" Len asked.

"I don't know."

"Remember him when we were freshmen? Seemed an okay guy then. But what's he getting at— talking about death. With you in the room."

"I guess he likes to be timely, you know?" Jim was unable to keep the bitterness out of his voice.

"That's heavy, man." He clapped Jim on the shoulder and went on down the hall.

Jim watched Len's easy stride. Of all the guys on

the team, he thought, he had the most respect for Len. He was close to Bud Alden, had known him all his life. And most of the other guys were great to hang around with. But Len he respected. Maybe it was because you could never really get close to Len, but you knew he was always there the way he was that day last season. Maybe that's what it was.

It was late fall, the season was nearly over. They were playing the last game, the one that would give them a chance at State. But they were up against the Milrose Tigers, a team well named. The Tigers were five yards from paydirt, but Woods Cross had held them play after play. Then they fumbled, and Len scooped up the ball.

He was surrounded and he knew it. Jim stood alone a few feet away, so Len tossed him the ball. It happened so quickly, Jim had no time to think. He tucked the ball under his arm and began to run. He felt hands gripping his thighs, tugging at him, but he swerved and shook them off. He saw Gardner near him, pacing him, his hands out to receive. He thought about passing, knowing Gardner was the best player on the team and had a clear field in front of him. But Jim hung on to the ball and dove through the opposing team's line like a bull at a gate. He thought only of the goalpost and the woods beyond. He ran for those woods.

When he crossed the goal line, he didn't stop. In the woods he threw himself on the ground, panting, but weeping with joy. I've shown them, he thought. I've shown them there's more than one Halbert in the family.

The guys made a chair of their arms and carried him back across the field to the uproar of cheering from the stands. They reached the bench, and there was Jake, his face vermillion.

"Put him down," Jake said, "and get back out there. You've got a game to play."

Jim had stood grinning at his father, then started out behind his teammates.

"Where do you think you're going?"

"Back out to the field. To make the kick."

"You make it, boy, and then you get your butt back here. You're benched, you goddamned Saturday hero."

Jim missed the kick and spent the rest of the game on the bench, watching in misery. They won the game by six points—his six points, he told himself.

He didn't ask his father why he'd been benched, but he made up his mind about one thing. He wasn't coming back the next year.

"Man," Len said when he told him, "you can't do that. Next year's the big one—our senior year."

"I can't take it, Len. He yells at me all the time, but today really takes it. Hell, I ran ninety-five yards. And he jumps all over me."

"Yeah, I know. That was tough. I don't know why he did that, man."

"I'm not going back. I won't be his whipping boy anymore, Len."

"Look, maybe he's a little hard on you because you're his kid, but he yells at everybody. Look at Alden. He spends so much time on the bench, he's got slivers in his ass. And he doesn't talk about quitting."

"It's different for Bud. Bud has a, well, a thing about Dad. A kind of hero worship."

"Don't we all? Coach is the meanest cat in town, but he's got it together. He knows how to make you mad—mad enough to kill—and that's what makes us play the way we do. He keeps us together, makes us work like a fine machine. Hell, you made that run because you were mad as hell. I saw it in your eyes when I threw you the ball. I knew you'd take it in, man. I knew it."

"But, Len, why does he talk to me like that? It's worse than the others. You know it is."

Then Len told him about how Jake needed him. Jim didn't understand that, but he knew somehow there was a truth in it. It took the wind out of his sails, but he still felt trapped.

Now he had the same feeling again. But it wasn't his father this time, it was Dundee. Jim wished he'd gone on with Len. Maybe Len would know how to help him through this one, too.

4

The lunchroom was crowded, but finally Jim picked out Mimi. Holding his lunch tray, he headed toward her. He had expected to find her at one of the small tables near the window where they could talk quietly. Instead she was at the head of one of the large tables, surrounded by a group of kids. Bud Alden was among them.

"Here he is now!" Mimi announced, gesturing to an empty chair on her right. "We were just talking about you."

"Oh?" Jim sat down, muttering hello to the crowd and trying to show by his expression how annoyed he was with Mimi for not being alone.

"We're forming a conspiracy," one of the girls said. "And you're part of it."

"A conspiracy of honor," Mimi said. "I like that. We're going to make Woods Cross the most important school in the whole state. And we're going to make this year the most important one Woods Cross has ever known."

"Hear, hear!" said one of the boys.

"And how are you going to do that?" Jim asked, unable to keep the bitterness from his tone.

"Well, first we're going to get after the creeps in the school—the guys who break the rules and write on the walls. And we're going to remind them what this school means this year. How important it is and all," Mimi said.

Jim could see she really meant what she was saying.

"Good luck!" said one of the boys, but he was hooted down by the others.

"We are! We're going to make this the best school in the whole state. And you"—she beamed at Jim—"you're going to be the best football player in the state. That's your job."

"Oh, is that all? Well, that'll be a piece of cake. No sweat."

"I mean, you already are the best, of course, but you're going to be even better. I mean, this is the year for it. Our senior year and—and his last year. We want him to know how much he means to us."

Jim felt as if all the air had been knocked out of him. "Who?" he asked.

Mimi reached over and squeezed his hand. Her own was wet with perspiration. "Coach. Your dad. We're doing it for him. It's our special tribute."

Bud lifted his milk carton in a toast. "To the greatest guy in the world—and the meanest bastard who ever lived."

Jim looked at his friend and saw Bud's almost angelic face. The others laughed and raised their own cartons in salute.

Mimi was still holding Jim's hand. "I'm sorry I was such a jerk earlier," she said. "I mean, I couldn't take it all in, about your dad and everything. But I've got it together now. I'm so proud, Jim. Proud to be your girl." She learned over and kissed him on the cheek. Then she began to eat, smiling up at him between bites.

Jim would not look at her, or at any of them. He ate in silence, while around him they bubbled with their plans. This was the Mimi he'd ached for all summer? This was the girl he was going to pour it all out to, who would understand his pain and the shame he felt?

On his way to the locker room Jim saw Liz standing in an alcove with her back to him. He was about to poke his sister playfully in the ribs when he realized she was crying.

"Hey, Lizzy, what's wrong?"

She turned her head and blinked away the tears. "Nothing." She stopped to pick up her books. "I—I was just looking for something."

"Where? On the wall?"

"Oh, Jim," she wailed, all pretense gone. "It's so awful. I didn't think it would be like this."

"What's awful, Lizzy? School?"

"Yes. The kids. The way they treat me. It's just awful."

"Treat you? I don't understand." Liz was not one of the kids who was teased or unpopular.

"About Dad. Ever since they heard about him. They—they treat me so carefully, trying not to say anything, but looking at me. Even Sue Alden. At lunch she'd saved a seat for me, but she had some other kids there too, and they talked so quietly, like they were at a funeral or something. But that's not the worst part."

"What is, baby?"

"The way they whisper about me behind my back. I went into the girls' bathroom, and a couple of girls in my homeroom were talking about me. I heard my name and then when they saw me, a big hush. They won't look at me, but when I go past they're staring. Even the teachers. They keep looking at me. I just hate it. I don't want to go back, not ever."

He slipped his arm around her shoulders and let her lean against him. Somehow in his preoccupation with his own problems during the day he forgot about Liz, that she might be going through the same thing.

Some boys passed, punching each other and shouting.

Liz drew away quickly. "I—I guess I'd better go on home. I don't want to, though," she added, more to herself.

"Want to come and watch practice?"

"Football? I—I don't know. It's been a long time since I watched."

Jim remembered Liz on the bleachers, a permanent feature of the afternoon practices when he was a freshman. And before, when they were both at middle school, sometimes they'd come over and watch and afterward Jake would take them home. Bud Alden, too, and the four of them would sing old songs and laugh. It had been a good time for the most part. That had gone; it had slipped away with growing up.

"I could drive you home afterward."

Liz glanced at her watch. "I've already missed my bus. I don't mind. I can do my homework while I watch. Thanks, Jim."

The locker room was empty. Jim changed quickly into his uniform and went out onto the field. The team was warming up, stretching and doing jumping jacks. Coach had not yet appeared, so Len was leading them. They knew better, Jim thought, than to sit waiting. He joined them.

He could see Liz settling on the bleachers, and farther down the field, Mimi and her cheerleaders. Mimi was facing him, her hands on her hips. Then she turned and began a leaping cheer, almost in mimicry of the boys' jumping jacks.

"Okay, you clowns, get your butts over here!" Jake's voice cut the crisp fall air like a knife. "You look like a bunch of queers leaping about like that. Like those girls over there."

"We were just warming up," Len said, "instead of waiting."

"Who gave you the job of coach, boy?" Jake flared.

Jim saw Len's eyes flicker, but he kept his mouth rigid, his head erect.

"And when you have to wait"—Jake turned to the others—"you wait here, on the bench, understand? I don't want to use my strength to get you guys back in order. Is that clear?"

Jim could hear the resentment in the ragged breathing of the boys near him. If they'd waited, Coach would have yelled at them for not getting warmed up.

Jake lined them up and walked along like a top sergeant inspecting his troops. When he got to Jim, he stopped. He put his hands on his hips and stared at him, eye to eye because they were the same height. Jim realized suddenly that his father had not looked at him all summer, nor had they spoken more than a few words. Jim forced himself to keep his eyes forward, staring unblinking at his father.

"So you decided to join us, did you, Halbert? Nice you could make it."

"Yes, sir."

"I suppose you haven't forgotten the way we play this game?"

"No, sir."

"As if you ever knew," he spat out, then moved on down the line.

Len and Jim exchanged weak smiles. *The year is off and flying,* Len's eyes said. *Coach hasn't changed a bit.*

The plays were basic today, nothing spectacular. It was two weeks before the first preseason scrimmage, and Jake was testing their mettle. There were a lot of contact drills. Jim was tired and battered when Jake called a halt and sent them to the bleachers for the last speech of the day.

They settled back, knowing what to expect. They wouldn't be praised, even though they'd had a good session. Jake never praised them, not in these speeches after a drill, nor after a winning score. In fact, even when he spoke at the awards banquet after he'd taken the team to State, there was no praise. For eleven years now, Jake had accepted the trophy with a grunt of thanks and had told the assembled parents he'd won that year—and every year—in spite of the team, not because of it. Then he took the trophy home and put it in the basement den—the "game room," as it had come to be called.

Jim often wondered what it was about his father that held the team together. He knew that in spite of

the way Jake chewed them out, the players idolized
him. "I'd follow him through hell," a boy had once
told him. For Jim, that's just what it was—hell.

He knew, of course, it had something to do with
pride. Though Jake never gave them the credit they
deserved, the Woods Cross team was a proud team.
He guessed somehow his father had made it that way.

Len nudged him. "What do you think? Think
we've got a team?"

"What? Oh, I don't know. Seemed weak today."

"Seemed weak all summer. I think we're a washout this year."

"It's still early, Len."

"Look around. You see any big guys? Any
power?"

Jim saw what Len meant. Bud Alden was directly
behind him. He averted his gaze when Jim looked his
way. Bud was the smallest member of the team, but
the other boys were not much bigger. Last year they'd
had Gardner, who weighed well over 200 pounds. But
this year, no one even came close. Too many of them
were sophomores, eager and excited to have made the
team, but not fully grown yet, not ready.

"I see what you mean. But Coach'll shape them up.
He always does," Jim said.

"Yeah. But I'm not so sure this year. He seems to
be going through the motions, but not really with it.
Can't blame him of course." Len's eyes met Jim's for a

moment. "Anyway, it's good to have you back, man. 'Cause you're our Great White Hope." He grinned.

"Me? You got to be kidding, Len. If I'm your Great White Hope, you're in big trouble."

Jake was still on the field. Two of the boys were standing with him. Jake's voice, strident but muffled by the rising breeze, came across toward them. The boys seemed to grow smaller and Jake larger with each word, like shadows changing in the setting sun. Jake was holding the football against his chest, curled in his arm. He grabbed it with his left hand and held it high.

Then he threw the ball. It spun in the air, eclipsing the sun for a moment, and the boys scurried after it. The toss was high and wide. They couldn't get near it before it bounced crazily. One of them threw himself on the ground, but the ball, with a life of its own, scuttled away.

Jake's voice came again. "No, no, no, you—" Then it faded as he turned and started to run.

An airplane buzzed overhead, flying low. Jim squinted against the sunlight and looked up. The plane glimmered silver in the sky. For a moment he was in that small plane, buzzing over the field, over the town—the all-consuming Woods Cross merely a dot of trees and flattened houses.

A great hoot came from the field. Just Jake hollering again, Jim thought, but the sound was different, like no shout of Jake's Jim had ever heard before. It was like the cry of a great beast in pain. Jake was no longer running. He was lying facedown on the field.

"My God," Len said under his breath, and the team poured off the bench onto the field.

Jim hesitated, gathering his wits. He was slow to get up, and when he did, the team had huddled around Jake. By the time Jim reached him, Jake was on his feet, held on either side by a boy.

"Will you clowns let go of me?" Jake said, cuffing at them.

But the boys still held him. Jim could tell from the way Jake leaned against them that if they let go, he would topple. Jim stood there as if paralyzed. He knew he should step forward, say something to comfort his father instead of gaping at him, but he was unable to move.

His arm was gripped from behind. "Jim, what's wrong? What's happened?" It was Liz.

"Come on," Jim said, and together they hurried forward.

Jake shook off the two boys, and staggering a bit, regained his footing. "Now, what's all this crap?" he shouted. "Didn't I tell you clowns to stay on those bleachers, for Christ's sake?"

"Dad," Jim said, laying his hand on his father's shoulder. It was a strange sensation, seeing his hand there where it had never been and wondering why it was there.

Jake's eyes were small, squinting to see in the fading light of late afternoon. He was pale under the ruddy tan his outdoor life gave him, and sweat poured down his face. His eyes met Jim's.

Jim saw for a moment the flicker of weakness, like a small animal peering out from its hiding place and then scurrying away, unable to trust.

Jake flailed his arms, knocking Jim's hand aside. "Get away from me," he said directly to his son. Then he turned his head, taking in the rest of the boys. "All of you. What's with you? I trip on this goddamned turnip patch they call a football field, and you act like I'm a cripple. Get over to those bleachers like I told you."

Liz pushed past Jim and went to her father. "Daddy? Are you all right?"

"What? Little girl, what are you doing here?"

"I came to watch practice."

"That's right. You're at the school now. Hell, I'd forgotten." He went up to her and slipped his arm around her shoulders, an easy gesture of affection.

"Daddy, shouldn't we go home? It's getting dark."

"I guess so. That fall didn't do me much good." It was said quietly, privately. If Jim hadn't been standing there, he wouldn't have heard it. The other boys were drifting slowly back across the field. "It's just that I've got to whip these guys into shape. They're so goddamned weak."

Liz put her arm around her father's waist. Jim noticed how easily he leaned against her. There was no resistance. For a moment Jim felt jealous. Why couldn't he be easy with me like that. But then he knew it had always been that way with Liz.

"There'll be another practice, Dad. Tomorrow."

Jake sighed. "Yes, I guess so. Another practice."

Jim wanted to go to him, to put his arm around him from the other side. He took a step forward.

Jake looked up, realizing Jim was there. "I thought I told you to get over on the bleachers?" he roared.

"I—"

"Do I have to repeat myself, boy? Get over there where you belong."

Liz's eyes, bright in the darkness, met Jim's. "Tell them to go on home, Jim. Daddy's finished for tonight."

Jim ran across the field toward the bleachers where the team was standing around talking. He felt angry tears pushing into his eyes, but he fought them. Why was it so easy for Jake to take Liz's love and her pity, and not his?

Somehow, tonight, the closeness between Liz and Jake hurt Jim. He'd never felt that way before. He hoped he wouldn't feel that way ever again.

5

When Jim settled down to study, the first thing he came upon in his notebook was a tattered sheet of yellow paper. He was about to toss it into the wastebasket when his eye caught the sketches in the margin. Then he remembered that crazy girl who'd called herself Gus.

The sketches were very good; the math, what there was of it, sadly confused. She'd gotten only part of the assignment, had misspelled half the words, and dotted the page with question marks. He hung the paper on his wall with a piece of Scotch tape and got to work on his own math.

"But, Daddy"—his sister's voice whined in the hallway—"you shouldn't—"

"Now, don't tell me what I shouldn't do, little girl. You're getting as bad as your mother."

"But you're tired. You should lie down."

"I'll lie down soon enough, Lizzy."

Jim heard his father's steps receding down the hall and then a tentative knock on his door.

"Jim?" Liz's voice was strangely muffled.

"Liz? What's wrong?"

The door opened slowly. Liz peered around it shyly as if she hadn't been barging in on him since they were kids. "Am I interrupting?"

"Nothing important. Only homework."

"Oh." She began to close the door again.

He got up and pulled it open. "What's the matter?"

"It's Daddy," she said softly, coming into the room. She wore the same expression she'd had on the field and all through supper.

"What about Dad?"

"He—he insisted on going downstairs and riding that bicycle. He's down there now."

"Liz, he does that every night. You know that."

She lowered her head. He could see the crooked part running through her hair like a trail through a woods. "I know, but tonight . . ." Her voice trailed off.

He found himself defending his father, something he rarely did, even with Liz. "He has to, Liz. He has to go on as if nothing's different. It's his way." He had heard the words before, picked them up somewhere. They weren't his own. He was merely mouthing them, but somehow he wondered if they weren't exactly what he believed.

"But you didn't see him, Jim. I did. He's in pain. That's why he fell. He was running, and the pain was too much. He doubled over and then he fell. I think he's in pain most of the time."

Jim remembered the way his father had looked in the hall earlier. "I know," he said softly.

"Yet he goes on. As if nothing's changed. I can't stand it, Jim. I really can't."

"He has to go on, Liz. Like I said. That's how he is."

"Can't you stop him, Jim? Can't you do something?"

"Me? What can *I* do?"

"Talk to him. Tell him how it upsets us. Get him to slow down or something."

"You've got to be kidding, Liz. He won't listen to me."

"Well, he won't listen to me. And he won't listen to Mom. I've asked her to do something, and she just looks at me with that funny look she has. You know, like I've asked for a million dollars."

"Lizzy, you know how it is with Dad. Nobody can make him do what he doesn't want to do. Not Mom, not me, and I guess not even you."

"He should stay home and rest. He doesn't have to work, and he doesn't have to coach the team."

"Dad not coach? Liz—"

"No, wait. Up on the bleachers today I was sitting with Coach Griswold. You know, the freshman coach. I have him for gym, and we got to talking. He told me how much he thought of Dad. You know, things like that. And he told me how he'd offered to coach both teams this year. Dad wouldn't listen, though."

"I can imagine. Dad always said Griswold was after his job."

"Well, he's a nice guy, and it was a good idea. I mean, Dad shouldn't be staying late and running around the field and losing his temper. And"—her eyes filled with tears—"and riding that bicycle like that. What's he trying to prove?"

What's he trying to prove? Jim turned the question over in his mind, wondering if there was an answer. It was a question he'd asked himself all his life and now his sister gave voice to it.

"At least you could go down there and talk to him, couldn't you?"

He shrugged. "I could try. But it wouldn't do much good, and you know it."

"I wish he weren't at school. That's awful, I know, and I shouldn't say it, but I wish he weren't. I felt weird today just saying my name. In fact I mumbled it most of the time. Of course the freshmen don't know Dad, but the rumor was all over school, so of course, they ask. I really hated it. I dread going back."

She stared for a long time at the clock on Jim's desk, as if counting the seconds. Finally she said, "I'm sorry. I shouldn't have said that. I shouldn't think about myself now. But I can't help it, Jim. Going to high school is supposed to be such a great time. I've looked forward to it ever since you started. My freshman year. And then this had to happen. I know that's a rotten way to think of it, though. I feel just awful."

"Look, Liz, your first day of high school isn't over yet. You haven't been property initiated."

"Initiated? I don't understand."

"You haven't been to Mandy's."

She smiled, though her eyes still held their pain. "Mandy's? Only high school kids go to Mandy's."

"Well, then, what are you waiting for? Let's go."

"Are you serious? It's nearly eight-thirty. I don't think Mom'll like us taking off now, on a school night."

"Mom'll understand. Just let me finish my homework. I'll get this last trig problem solved and then we'll go."

He felt a little guilty deflecting Liz from the subject of their father that way. It was rather like offering a lost child an ice-cream cone. It didn't solve the real problem. But he had no idea how to solve that—not even for himself, let alone for Liz.

As Jim tried to study, his eyes kept wandering to the yellow paper on the wall. He thought about Gus

Palmer—her wide grin, her brusque manner. In the short time he'd sat with her, the burden of his father's sickness had lifted from him. Maybe Gus had a way of dispelling the air and with it the heaviness of living. Maybe she'd be good for Liz too. He knew going to Mandy's wasn't going to help all that much.

Gus probably did need that paper tonight. Maybe he could get it to her, drop it by or something. He went to his bedside table and took out the phone book. Then he remembered she said she was new in town. What else had she said—they lived over—what? The cheese shop. That would have to be West Avenue, the only main street in town. There was a cheese shop there, a few blocks from Mandy's.

Proud of his detective work, he dialed the number he'd gotten from directory assistance.

The phone was answered on the first ring by a boy. When Jim asked for Gus, the boy slammed down the receiver and bellowed, "Gussie! It's for you!"

Jim could hear a baby crying in the background and a man yelling.

"Yeah?" Gus answered.

"Uh, Gus, this is Jim Halbert."

"Who?"

"Jim Halbert. We—uh—we sat together in study today. For a while."

"Oh, yeah, sure. You're the good-looking guy with the sad eyes."

"What?"

"How you doing? You know, they really gave me a bad time today. I got kicked out right and left. I'll never get the hang of that school."

"I called because you left your math assignment on the table. I have it."

"No kidding? Jesus. I'd given up on that totally. I looked all the hell over the place for it. I thought I'd lost it. Gee, aren't you nice. I mean, that's really a nice thing to do, calling me up to tell me."

He pulled the paper off the wall and smoothed it with his hand. "I wondered if you'd like me to drop it by."

"Drop it by? Here? Oh. Gee, Jim, it's a bad time. My dad is tearing the place to hell." The voice in the background was still roaring. "He's had a bad day, you know?"

Without thinking, Jim said, "I know." Then quickly he added, "I—I'm going over to Mandy's in a few minutes. That's just at the corner of West and Willow. Not far from the cheese—I mean, from where you live. Maybe you could meet me."

"Mandy's? That little coffee shop?"

"Yes. Do you know it?"

"Yeah, I've been there. Okay. I've got to get out of here anyway. See you there."

After he'd hung up, Jim felt better. Even hearing Gus's breathless voice over the phone lifted his spirits.

He finished his math and glanced over his assignment notebook. Under English he'd scrawled "What D. Means to Me." It took him a moment to remember what that meant, then the full impact of it came down on him like a heavy weight, crushing his spirit. Dundee and his damned probing. He closed the notebook and grabbed his jacket, but the thought stayed in his mind like a bad taste in his mouth.

6

Mandy's stood like a sentry house at the corner of West and Willow, the only lighted building on the street of shops. Jim pulled his Volkswagen into a parking space beside an old Buick. Mandy's was the hangout for the high school crowd as the condition of the cars attested.

"I've only been here once," Liz was saying. "Once after practice Dad drove us over here, remember?"

"It's not such a big deal. I mean, it's a dirty little place run by a dirty old man."

"I know. But it's like a milestone, you know? You just can't go to Mandy's until you get to high school."

Jim gripped her shoulder. "Welcome to high school, little sister." He kissed her lightly on the nose. Her eyes shone in the dark of the car.

Mandy himself—or at least the old man everybody assumed was Mandy—was wiping the counter with a dirty cloth. The place was full of kids, and the jukebox wailed a country and western song. Jim found a booth near the door, waved to a few people he knew, then went to the counter for the Cokes.

Once settled across from each other, they seemed to have little to say. Liz had fallen into silence, and Jim found he was getting depressed. It had probably been a mistake to come to Mandy's. Then he remembered Gus.

"I'm meeting someone here in a while."

"Oh? Mimi?"

"No. A girl from school. I went off with her math assignment. I told her I'd bring it here. I hope you don't mind."

Liz shrugged. "Why should I mind? I'm glad it's not Mimi, though."

"What's wrong with Mimi?"

"Nothing, I guess. But, I don't know, she's so— oh—so pretty."

Jim laughed. "So what's the matter with that?"

"Nothing. It's just that it seems like that's all she is—pretty. I guess when you're that pretty, it's enough." She finished her Coke, her brow furrowed with concentration.

"Want another?" he asked.

"Yeah, sure."

Jim ordered two more Cokes and leaned against the counter staring at the filthy green walls. He had no idea why Mandy's stayed so popular. There was a

new McDonald's at the other end of West Avenue and
a Burger King just off the state highway. But Mandy's
kept the business.

Suddenly the door flew open and crashed against
the paperback rack. Jim turned, somehow knowing
who it was. Who else but Gus could make an entrance
like that?

She was wearing the same clothes she'd worn to
school—tight jeans that clung to her long legs and a
tie-dyed shirt. She grinned when she saw him.

"Hey, right on the money, Halbert," she said. She
perched on a stool at the counter, slung a beaded
shoulder bag onto the counter top, and extracted a
pack of cigarettes. Mandy brought Jim the two Cokes
he'd ordered. "These both for you?" Gus asked.

"No. One of them's for my sister, Liz." He
pointed at the booth.

"Hey, she's pretty." Then she narrowed her eyes.
"You wouldn't be putting me on, would you? About
her being your sister."

"No. Why should I do that?"

Gus stuck a cigarette between her thin lips and
lighted it. "Just kidding. I can be very jealous, you
know."

Jim laughed somewhat nervously. He tried to read
Gus's expression, but her eyes were squinting against
the smoke from her cigarette. He hoped she was kidding, but he wasn't sure. He began to wonder what

he'd gotten himself into. Because he called her, did she think—?

"I'll have one of those Cokes too," Gus was telling Mandy. "Just bring it over to that end booth." She picked up her bag, draped it over her shoulder, and turned.

"No table service," Mandy muttered.

"What?"

"I said no table service. You pick up here. Take it to the table yourself."

Gus leaned against the counter and drew a long drag on her cigarette. Then, just as slowly, she blew the smoke out directly into Mandy's face. "You're making a mistake," she said softly, an edge of threat in her voice.

Jim lingered, wishing he'd never called this crazy girl. He had no idea what she was going to do, but he remembered the scene in study hall with Mrs. Linden. Was she going to be chucked out of Mandy's too?

"No table service," Mandy said again. "You still want a Coke?"

"Yeah. But you're making a mistake." The threat was gone from Gus's voice. "McDonald's can do it this way. You can't. You'll lose business."

Mandy shrugged. "So, I lose business. A lot of bums who don't eat. Just drink Coke."

"That's what I mean. Kids with no money—that's what you get. Now, if you fixed the place up a little and hired someone to wait tables, why, in no time—"

"You want this Coke or not?"

"Sure. Look, I'll catch you later. We can talk about it, okay?"

"Yeah, sure." Mandy went back to wiping the counter.

Jim looked at Liz. She was watching, her eyes wide with surprise. At least she couldn't accuse Gus of being too pretty, he thought ruefully. Gus picked up her Coke and they went over to the booth. Settled across from Liz, Gus stuck out her hand. Liz took it gingerly, the surprise still on her face.

"Jim here says you're his sister. That right?"

"Uh, yes. Liz Halbert."

"Pleased to meet you. You're got some great brother here, you know?"

"Oh? What makes you think so?"

"Hell, here I go off and leave my math assignment in study, and he calls me up and comes over here with it."

Jim reached in his pocket and took out the folded sheet of yellow paper. "I'm afraid it doesn't make much sense," he apologized, as if it were his fault. "But here is it."

"It doesn't make much sense to me either," Gus said. "But I'll give it a whirl. They say I need this stuff to graduate. How I'm going to graduate is a mystery to me. But I gotta. My old man said this is it. If I don't make it this year at this school, then I've had it." She stubbed out her cigarette and took a long sip of Coke.

"Do you go to Woods Cross?" Liz asked.

"Yeah. My first day. Nearly my last."

"Really? But you're not a freshman."

"No, I'm a senior. But we just moved here. From West Virginia. I tell you, I was lost most of the time. And when I wasn't lost, I was getting in trouble. Me and W.C. just ain't going to make it, I'm afraid." She began to rummage in her beaded bag again and brought out a crumpled piece of paper. "Look at this, will you?" She smoothed it out on the table. "I'm on probation. First day, and already I'm on probation."

"What'd you do to get that? Not just because you talked in study?"

"Oh, no. I went on to bigger and better things after that. I improved my act considerably. For starters I was late to every class. And I got caught smoking in the girls' lav. And I talked out in science. Let's see, what else?" She studied the paper for a while, then shrugged. "But why am I bothering you guys with my troubles? You're the only people who've been nice to me all day. Ever since I came to this town, in fact, I've felt like some sort of freak. Everybody's so hoity-toity. Except for you." She turned her gaze fully on Jim.

He squirmed. It made him uncomfortable to be admired so openly. He fingered the edge of the math paper, then spread it out. "Maybe I can get you started on this."

"Hey, I was hoping you'd say that." She reached once more into her beaded bag and this time produced an algebra book.

"You've got everything in there. I expect you to come up with a live rabbit next."

"Yeah. It's a regular carpetbag. Everything I own comes out of it. Fancy, a southerner bringing a carpetbag north."

Liz was looking at the drawings on the math paper. "Did you draw those?" she asked.

"Yeah, I always doodle when I get bored. And I get bored a lot. Especially in math." She opened her book to a page that, like the paper, was covered with sketches. "This is the page we did today."

"Yes, I can tell," Jim said.

She glanced up, her eyes sharp, ready to flare up, but she caught his grin. "Yeah, I guess I know what you mean. My pencil just starts in. Can't help it. So, if you can just get me started on this assignment, I won't take up any more of your time."

Jim bent over the book, trying to explain algebra to Gus. It was hopeless. She had no concept of what algebra was about and wasn't too clear on basic math. "You'll have to talk to Mr. Bowden," he said at last. "Maybe they'll let you take a semester of pre-algebra first."

"But if I do that I won't graduate on time, right?"

Jim nodded.

"Geez, I feel like I've landed on this earth newborn but fully grown. I'm behind before I begin."

"Woods Cross just isn't set up for new students, I guess. We're not used to—I mean, just about everybody there has gone through middle school here, too."

"Yeah, so I noticed. Trouble with this town is you got to be born here. My town in West Virginia was like that, too. I guess I was pretty smug back there." She took out her package of cigarettes and lit one. "Anyway, I got to get through this year and get a diploma. And I got to figure out these xs and ys to do it. Maybe I'll talk to Mr. Bowden. He seems like a regular guy. But I've got to try on this one assignment first. Otherwise he'll stick me in that pre-algebra for sure."

The door behind them opened again, sending a draft into the room. Jim looked up, and there was Mimi.

She was laughing with a girl friend over some private joke. Then she saw Jim. She motioned to her friend, and the girl nodded and went on to the back of the room. Mimi came over. She opened her mouth to speak, but when she saw Gus sitting next to Jim, dragging on a cigarette and squinting at the algebra book, Mimi froze, her mouth still open but no words coming out.

Jim didn't speak either, though he started to get up.

Mimi's blue eyes flashed. "Excuse me," she said. "I

thought you were somebody I knew." She spun on her heel and joined her friend in the back.

"Wasn't that—" Liz began, but Jim hushed her.

Gus had been so absorbed, she didn't seem to notice. "Okay," she said, raising her head, "I think I get this part—about *x* being what you want it to be."

"Not what you want it to be, Gus. What you guess it is."

"Yeah, okay. But why are these numbers in parentheses and these others aren't?"

Jim leaned over the book and tried to concentrate, but his mind screamed at him to get up and go find Mimi. Don't let her sit there thinking he's out with Gus on some kind of date. Because that must be exactly what she thought, otherwise why would she have gotten angry all of a sudden?

He looked at Gus, trying to see her as Mimi had. She was too thin. Her arms were like matchsticks, and her T-shirt clung to her small pointed breasts. She was a far cry from Mimi's round softness. Her mouth was too wide for her long face and her eyes too small. She was nothing like Mimi, and yet he could see what Mimi must have seen. In a rough, unfinished sort of way, she was sexy. He had to admit he was drawn to her, even aroused.

Gus looked up. "What are you gaping at?" she asked.

He reddened. "Nothing."

He thought about what she'd said, how she had to graduate or that was it. He remembered the crying baby when he'd called, and the man shouting. Maybe he just felt sorry for her, nothing more.

"Look, I've got an idea. Why don't I do that assignment for you? That'd get you off the hook."

"Hell, you can't do that."

"It wouldn't take me more than a few minutes, Gus. I could get it to you before your class and then you could talk to Mr. Bowden about extra help."

"But if you do it, it'll be perfect and then he'll think I do understand." She shook her head. "Nope, it just won't work. Even if I did let you do it, which I won't. I may not be much compared to you Woods Cross types, but I don't cheat."

Stung at the rebuff, Jim lowered his head.

"Jim doesn't cheat, either," Liz said firmly. "He wasn't talking about cheating."

"What then?" Gus flared. "I can't let him do my work. And I can't do it myself. So I'm up a creek without a paddle." She pronounced it "crick," which made Liz laugh.

Jim pushed his Coke aside. "Look, I get what you mean. I was just offering to give you a hand this time to get you out of a tough spot. I'll make a few mistakes and then you can talk to Mr. Bowden. If you go in with nothing done, you'll land in pre-algebra for sure."

"Yeah, you're right about that." Gus studied the paper, now covered with numbers and letters as well as drawings, making it more of a muddle than ever.

"I could give you some help during study, too."

"Oh! We tried that, remember?"

"I can talk to Mrs. Linden. She'll let us if we're quieter."

"Why?"

"Why what?"

"Why should you do all this? I mean, you keep my paper instead of throwing it away, you call me up, and now you want to help me out. It's the nicest thing that's happened to me since I came to this town, but I don't get it."

That set Jim to wondering about it too. He didn't usually go out of his way to help people, even his friends. Why now? Why Gus?

Then her eyes narrowed. "You wouldn't be offering me charity, would you?"

"Charity?"

"Yeah. Helping me out because you feel sorry for me or something."

He reddened.

"We Palmers don't accept charity, not from anyone. My dad only came here because his army buddy offered him a job. And we pay good money for that crummy room over the cheese shop. Whatever people say, we ain't on welfare."

Taken back by the fervor of her speech, Jim could only stare, searching for words.

Liz was the one who spoke. "Gus, Jim wasn't offering you charity. He's helping you out because he likes you—as a friend. That's all."

Jim looked at his sister in gratitude, not only for placating Gus but for answering his own doubts. He was helping Gus because she was a friend, nothing more.

"All the same," Gus said, "I can't have you doing something for me if I can't do back. That's how we Palmers are."

"Well, maybe sometime you can do something for me, Gus." He slid the math book over and closed it.

Just then Mimi went up to the counter and spoke to Mandy, leaning against the stool, one leg up, her trim bottom snug in designer jeans.

Jim took a quick gulp of his Coke. "I'll be right back," he said, sliding out of the booth.

Mimi glanced around as he approached, a tiny frown line creasing her clear brow.

"Hi, baby," he said.

"Hello." Her tone was not exactly cold, but guarded. "I didn't expect to see you tonight—first night of school and all."

"I—uh—didn't expect to be here. Liz—my sister—was feeling a little low, so I brought her to Mandy's. It's her first year at Woods Cross, so it's kind of a tradition."

"Liz has changed," Mimi said sarcastically. "Lost some weight."

"That's not Liz. That's Gus Palmer. You know, the girl who came late to study today? She's new to Woods Cross. From West Virginia." He didn't know why he was talking in staccato sentences, or why he was talking about Gus at all.

"So you're the official welcoming committee." She picked up her Coke and started past him.

He caught her arm. "Mimi, come on. It doesn't mean anything. I had her math paper and I called her to pick it up. She lives near here, above the cheese shop—" He stopped, taking in Mimi's doubtful expression. "Hell, it's too complicated to go into, but it doesn't mean anything. She's just a friend." Out of the corner of his eye he saw Gus slide out of the booth. He didn't want her to come over, not while he was talking to Mimi. "Uh, look, Mimi, I'll call you. We'll sort it all out, okay?"

She, too, had seen Gus stand up. She narrowed her eyes and replied, "Whatever you say." She flipped her hair and strode off to join her friends.

Gus put her foot up on the seat and lit another cigarette. She looked like a cowgirl in her jeans and tie-dyed T-shirt.

What the hell am I doing? Jim asked himself, glancing over at Mimi.

"I don't feel right about you doing my math for

me," Gus said when he joined them. "I was telling Liz here that there must be some way I could pay you back."

"I'll think of something," he said gruffly. "Want a ride home?"

"Sure, if it's not out of your way. I just live down the street, though. Over the—"

"Yeah, I know. The cheese shop. So you keep telling me."

"What's bugging you?" she asked.

"Nothing. I'm sorry, Gus. I'm just tired, I guess." They went out onto the street. "First day of school's always a trip, you know?"

"Do I ever. Man." He held the car door for her. Liz scrambled into the back, and Gus got in front. "Look, I've been thinking about it. I'll let you do that algebra for me. But you've got to let me do something for you. Otherwise it's no go."

"I told you I'd think of something."

"No, I mean now. Something tonight." She acted as if he were the one asking for a favor.

"I've done all my homework, Gus, and anyway—"

"And anyway, you think I couldn't do any of yours. That I'm too dumb."

"I didn't say that."

"Yeah, but you were thinking it. I'm not dumb, though, whatever you hoity types think. I can draw and I can write."

Jim remembered the one part of his homework he hadn't done—Dundee's theme. "You can write?"

"Yeah. You may not believe it, but I'm pretty good. It's half in my mind to be a writer someday. Why, you got some writing needs doing?"

"As a matter of fact I have this theme, but it's kind of a crazy subject."

"The crazier the better."

"It's about death. 'What death means to me.' "

"Death?" Liz said from the back. Jim could see her white face in the rear-view mirror.

Gus wrinkled her brow, thinking about it. "Sure, why not? Anybody die recently—in your family, or anything?"

He wet his lips before he answered. Liz looked at him, then looked away. "No," he said quietly, "no one."

"Well, I'll just make it kind of general. I'm getting some ideas already."

"Gus, try—try to make it, well, I don't know— sound like me, okay? I mean, I wouldn't want Dundee to know I didn't write it."

She laid her hand on his. "Trust me, Halbert. You take care of the math, and I'll take care of this theme." Then she smiled—that wide slash of a mouth across her thin face.

For a moment, Jim thought, she was almost pretty.

7

Jim lay in bed thinking about the free day stretching ahead of him. It was Saturday morning. He'd survived two days of school and things seemed to be fitting into a groove. Except, of course, for Mimi.

That brought him up sharply. As he helped Gus with her math in study, he kept feeling Mimi's eyes boring into his back. But when he looked around, she seemed to be reading. After study, she left without a word. He looked for her in the cafeteria at lunch, but she wasn't there. He knew he'd better call her, but not just yet.

He got out of bed, slipped on his robe, and went into the kitchen. His mother was chopping onions. The pungent smell made his eyes smart.

"Well," she said, "you had a good long sleep. It's nearly eleven."

"What are you up to?"

"Putting together a meat loaf. I'm going out for

lunch with Mrs. Johnstone, and I don't want to be fussing about dinner."

Jim opened the refrigerator and reached absently for the carton of milk. It wasn't there.

"There's some downstairs, dear. I have to get the grocery shopping done sometime today."

"I'll do the shopping, Mom. Just leave me a list."

She looked up from her work, her eyes red-rimmed from weeping. Jim was moved by her tears. He almost put his arms around her to comfort her, but then she laughed and said, "Pesky onions," and went on chopping.

Jim went downstairs to the game room.

There was no ping-pong table or billiards in the game room. It was really a den with an old couch, a chair, and the television set where Jake and sometimes boys from the team watched "Monday Night Football." It had come to be called the game room because of the trophies.

Every trophy Jake had ever won, from high school through college and the team trophies from his years of coaching, were lined up on shelves along one wall. Across from them, as if contemplating those gleaming tributes to a hero, was a painting of the hero himself, holding a football under his arm and dressed in the uniform of Penn State.

As far back as Jim could remember, he'd been fascinated by those trophies. He remembered a rainy day when he was very small. He'd been playing with his toys on the carpet. Suddenly the sun broke through the clouds enough to send a beam into the room. Jim looked up and saw a magic trail, alive with tiny specks. He'd followed the trail with his eyes and at the end of it was the greatest wonder of all—a golden football floating in the air. He'd squatted on his haunches and craned his neck, seeing for the first time the wall of golden cups with football players on top. Each player held a miniature ball, caught forever at the beginning of a forward pass.

Nowadays he hardly glanced at them when he came in the room, and he only came down here when he had to.

He could hear the whir of Jake's stationary bicycle. He hadn't realized his father was there, or he wouldn't have come. He hesitated outside the doorway, wondering if he should forget about the milk. But his mother would ask about it if he came up empty-handed. Maybe he could pass through without disturbing his father.

As he stepped into the room, the squeak of the bicycle ceased, and his father emitted a low grunt. Jim felt an unaccountable sense of panic. He forced himself to make his expression cheerful, even distracted, as if he were thinking of his errand and not aware his father was there.

Jake started up the bicycle once more. Relieved,

but ashamed, Jim went quickly to the refrigerator, got the milk, and headed toward the door.

"Who's there?" Jake called, bringing the bicycle to a halt.

"Uh, just me, Dad. Getting some milk."

Jake turned on the seat of the bicycle. Perspiration poured down his face, and his hair was dark with it. He had a white towel around his neck. His complexion was flushed and his eyes glittered. He struggled to get off the bicycle, paused, then tried again. He gripped the handlebars so tightly his knuckles were white. Jim took a step forward to help, but something in his father's manner made him stop.

"Goddamned thing," Jake muttered. "Either it's gotten taller or my leg's gotten shorter."

"Here, let me." Jim hurried over, put the milk on top of the TV and offered his shoulder to his father. For a moment Jake hesitated, grumbling to himself, then finally accepted Jim's help.

As his father leaned against him, Jim was suddenly aware of how light his father was. His frame was still large, the bulk was still there, but it was illusory.

Jake slid to his feet and slapped his son on the back. "Thanks, boy. I'll have to adjust that seat. I think I have it set too high. It's getting harder and harder to get off the damned thing."

The sweat glistened on his face, giving him a healthy glow—yet it was not health Jim saw in the deep-set eyes and the grayish pallor of his father's skin. "Should you—I mean, the bicycle's quite strenuous. Maybe you shouldn't ride it so much." He stopped just short of saying "anymore."

Jake leaned with one hand on top of the TV, wiping his face with the towel. "Not ride the old bike? Why the hell not?"

"I—I don't know, Dad. It just seems that, well—"

"Look, boy." Jake wiped the towel across his face once more, seeming to wipe the good humor off as well as the sweat. "I'm a fighter, you know? You've known your old dad long enough to have figured that out, haven't you?"

"Sure, Dad. But—"

"I don't quit. Jake Halbert didn't get where he is by quitting. Come over here, boy. Let me show you something."

They stood in front of the trophies. "See those, boy?"

"Of course, Dad."

"Yeah, I know. You've seen 'em all your life. They've been down here as long as you've been around, gathering dust. Your mother won't touch 'em, says she's afraid she'll break them." He ran a finger along the rim of one cup and came up with a grimy finger. "Yeah, they aren't much when you think about it. But they say something, Jim, something about your old man that I want you to remember." He paused, his voice shaking. "Your old man doesn't quit, you hear? He plays to win, no matter what the odds."

Jake leaned against him for a moment, his arm draped across Jim's shoulders. Jim was aware once more of how light his father was. Yet it was a dead weight, a weary weight, that leaned on him, leaned on him to keep from collapsing. When, regaining his footing, Jake clapped Jim on the arm and turned. "I don't want to hear any more about quitting, boy. You hear? Not the bike, not the team. Nothing."

He wrenched himself free of Jim's grasp and headed toward the door. Jim wondered about the sudden vehemence of his father's speech. It was as if he were trying to convince someone else, or maybe even himself.

Just before he went out the door, Jake turned again. "You know what they called me when I played in college?"

"Yes, Dad." He'd been told often enough, but somehow he didn't want to hear it now, not in this context.

"The killer," he said. "Jake the killer. Because I wouldn't stop. No matter what." He hurled the words into the air above him, perhaps to some demoralizing god thrown up as a challenge. "You coming upstairs, boy?"

"In a minute, Dad. I'll just get the milk."

Jim opened the milk carton and took a long swig. As he leaned his head back, tasting the cool thick liquid, his eyes fell on the painting. Like the trophies, it was part of his life, yet he had spent little time really looking at it.

A college friend of Jake's had painted it—Jake in his football jersey, holding his helmet in the circle of his arm. It looked uncannily like Jim himself, except for the bold thrust of the chin and the directness of the gaze. It was Jim's face without the softness, the uncertainty. It was the face of a hero—every bit his father.

Maybe it was the morning light filtering through the window, but there seemed to be a shadow in the eyes Jim had never noticed before. And there was a shading at the corners of the mouth as well, belying the heroic thrust of the chin. But in the eyes, there was almost—Jim blinked and looked again—was it fear? The younger Jake looked straight out of the picture, but there was fear in his eyes.

Jim remembered a book they'd studied in English last year—*The Picture of Dorian Gray*. It was about a man whose portrait grew old while the man stayed young. He finally hid the picture in the attic so that his friends wouldn't know the secret of his continued youth.

Was this Jake's portrait of Dorian Gray? While Jake remained the unconquerable hero, was the portrait, hidden here in the basement, taking on the fear, the weakness, the disease itself?

Quickly, before he was haunted by any more imaginings, Jim left the room. It was too early in the day for morbid thoughts.

8

Jim could just see the white of Mimi's hair and her face, like a full moon, cool and distant. She was sitting on the far edge of the seat, as far away from him as she could in a Volkswagen. She stared straight ahead and didn't speak.

"Want to go to a movie?" he asked.

She shrugged. "I don't care."

"Or drop by Mandy's?"

She shuddered as if cold. "No, not Mandy's. Definitely not Mandy's."

"McDonald's?"

"I suppose." Her voice was flat.

He headed toward the highway.

They were nearly to McDonald's when Mimi said, "No, never mind, Jim. I don't want to go there."

"Where then?" He was getting impatient.

"I don't want to be with people, to see people. Let's go somewhere where we can be alone."

He licked his lips. "The Gulley?"

She turned, her eyes flashing. "You just can't wait, can you?"

"Hey, Mimi, I just meant—if you want someplace quiet—"

"I'm sorry, Jim. I know you aren't like that. I'm just out of sorts tonight, that's all. Being my usual bitchy self." She smiled.

"I'll take you home if you want," he said.

"No, no, of course not." She snuggled up to him. "It's nice to be with you. It's been such a long time."

He put his arm around her and drove through the quiet streets of Woods Cross. It was the first time since summer began he'd felt really relaxed. He told her so.

"Me too. I mean, I've been so mixed up since I got back, you know? First I thought I didn't want to see you. Last weekend when I heard you'd called, I was sort of glad I was out. Because I didn't know what it'd be like to see you after all that time. Maybe you'd be different. Maybe I'd be different, I don't know. And then, when I got to school and heard about your dad, well, that really threw me, you know? I realized things wouldn't be the same—not like they were last year. Things like that, like your dad, well, they change things, you know? I guess I'm not making myself very clear."

Jim felt the peace breaking up. He didn't say anything, but loosened his hold on her shoulder.

"And then, the other night, going into Mandy's and seeing you with that—that person. I thought, oh-oh, this is it. You've lost him, Mimi-girl."

"You haven't, Mimi. Gus's just a friend. I'm helping her with math."

"Well, I know that now, of course. In fact, after I got home that night I thought about it. And it made me laugh. To think I could be jealous of her. I mean, look at her!" She began to giggle. "When Halloween comes, she won't even need a costume."

"She's not as bad as that, Mimi," he said coldly.

"No, I'm sorry. But you have to admit I was being silly. To think you'd throw me over for someone like that."

They were coming back into the main section of town now, nearing Mandy's. "Let's go there," Mimi said. "After all, it's our place. Maybe we can capture some of the old spirit."

As they passed the closed-up shops, Jim couldn't help glancing at the cheese shop. Then, almost guiltily, he looked at Mimi. "I've missed you," he said, "so much."

She smiled. "Me too. I've felt so out of it, you know? Everything seems to be passing me by, and I'm not really part of it. School, home—even you. I'm still in summer, drifting somewhere."

"On that lake, I suppose?"

He felt her tense against him. "Yes, I guess so," she said without enthusiasm.

Mandy's was quiet. Mandy himself, still wiping the counter, grunted when they entered. They picked a booth, and Jim brought Cokes.

"I wonder," Mimi said, "how much longer Mandy's will be here. I mean, it's falling to pieces. After we go, will kids still come here?"

"My sister will. Her crowd. Then there's others coming on up the line. I guess it'll always be here."

Mimi laughed and leaned back, relaxed at last. "Do you think he'll still be here? Years from now, still wiping the counter with that same dirty rag?"

"Centuries from now," Jim put in.

Mimi laughed again, the musical notes up the scale Jim remembered and liked. Then just as suddenly, her face became serious. "It's comforting in a way, you know."

"What is?"

"Mandy's. That it's here. That even the grease spot on the wall over the counter is still here—and will still be here years from now. It's like Woods Cross itself. It'll go on as it is. Nothing will change."

Jim sipped his Coke, and for some reason the image of his father bent over the bicycle in the game room came into his mind, his face as gray as his warmup suit. It wasn't true. Not everything will be the same. And if Jake was no longer part of Woods Cross, then Woods Cross would change beyond recognition.

Mimi had fallen silent. When she was thinking, her mouth turned down, almost in a pout.

"I hate change," she said at last. "You know that? I hated growing up, and now I hate the idea of getting old. Of graduating and leaving Woods Cross."

"You don't have to leave Woods Cross."

"Yes, but I probably will. I mean, I'll probably go east to college. Smith or somewhere. And then, who knows? And you'll go to Penn State or someplace."

"I don't know. I haven't really thought about it."

"You'll get a football scholarship. And besides, your dad's record will count a lot, won't it?"

Jim blushed. "I said I haven't thought about it," he said again, raising his voice.

"Sometimes I feel I want to reach out and grab on to a moment when it's passing, you know? Not let it slip by." She leaned back against the booth and gazed outward, her eyes fixed on some distant object, perhaps on the grease spot over Mandy's shoulder. "I always seem to grow up faster than everybody else, you know? Remember in middle school, how some of the girls have boobs already and others don't? Well, I was the first. Fifth grade and there I was, Bo Derek."

Jim remembered Mimi then. All the boys did.

"I hated it. I used to wish I was still a kid. I guess that's when I first started feeling this way.

"When I was a little girl," she went on, "I had a secret place I used to go to—a pond. You know how the Pinetum backs up on our property? I used to go there and sit by a pond for hours. There were frogs sometimes—I called it the frog pond—and they'd croak. It sounded like the twanging of a steel guitar string. It's funny, but whenever I get feeling low, I think about the frog pond."

"Want another Coke?"

She shook her head. "Wow, what got me started? No, no more. Let's get out of here. The place is giving me the creeps."

They drove in silence toward the highway once more. Jim hadn't consciously made the decision. He just kept driving and soon they were climbing the low hills, toward the Gulley.

It was the name given to a split in the hills that had been made into a small park by some civic-minded citizens right after the Second World War. In a flurry of patriotism they'd cleared a space, planted a lawn and tulips, and erected a statue to the war dead. Then they left it. Except for the statue, a soldier with a furled flag, and the annual return of the tulips, the park had returned to its scraggly natural self. But the road leading to it had opened the way into the woods and had become the favorite spot for lovers. On a Saturday night it was as full as a parking lot.

Mimi suddenly realized where they were headed. "Oh, Jim, no. I said no earlier."

"It—it's been so long, Mimi." His words sounded desperate to his ears, foolish.

"That's just the point," she said firmly. "It's been too long."

He was on the dirt road by that time, headed into the park.

"Jim, I said no."

"I can't turn around. I'll turn around in the Gulley." When he reached the first grove of trees, he saw three or four cars pulled in. He drove past the statue, the soldier looking blankly out. There was no place to turn around until they were deep in the grove. Finally he pulled into a small place under an oak. But he didn't turn around as he'd promised. He switched off the engine and faced Mimi.

Her face looked white and ghostly. He wanted to reach out and take that ghostly face in both his hands, test its reality. He wondered fleetingly if his hand would go right through it, like smoke. Her expression told him to go slowly.

"Mimi, let's just talk for a while. Nothing else."

"We tried talking. In Mandy's."

"You got depressed there. We didn't talk at all."

"I know. I don't know what happened. It felt—I don't know—so sad."

He moved closer and slipped his hand under her hair, gripping her neck in the old familiar way. She didn't resist. He drew her closer and was about to kiss her when he stopped, seeing a tear glistening on her cheek. "Mimi?"

She met his gaze, her eyes bright under the heavy

lashes. Then she flung herself into his arms. "Oh, Jim, hold me. Hold me. Make it all the way it was," she cried almost hysterically.

The heady smell of her perfume aroused him. He stroked her hair, his fingers responding to its silkiness. Then he kissed the top of her head, gently, like an uncle.

"Some things haven't changed, Mimi," he said quietly. "Like you said. Mandy's is still there. And we're still together. We're still good together." He felt her relax against him.

He brought his hand down her face, his fingers caressing the soft wet cheeks. He kissed her again, still gently. Her lips moved under his, opened. He brought his hand down across the full mound of her breasts, then up under her sweater, gripping the silk bra and the soft flesh.

She put both hands on his shoulders and pushed him away. Thinking she was teasing, he rolled up her sweater and kissed the firm breast where it spilled out of her bra. She pushed harder. "No, Jim."

He sat up. "Why not?"

She straightened her clothes and slid to the far side of the car. "I don't want to, that's all."

He remembered her tongue searching his mouth, the rise of her breasts as her breath quickened. "Yes you do, Mimi."

"I don't, Jim. Not—not tonight." She'd started to say something else.

"Not with me, you mean."

"I don't know. I don't know what I mean."

"Is there someone else, Mimi? Is that it?"

She turned her head swiftly, caught his gaze, then looked away. "No, not exactly."

"Not exactly? What's that supposed to mean?"

"Nothing. There's no one."

"What happened, Mimi? During the summer?"

"Happened? What makes you think anything happened?"

"Something did. I can tell. Something happened during the summer to change things."

She straightened her shoulders. "Well, for one thing, you never wrote. I mean, try that for starters."

"We went through all that before, Mimi. I told you—"

"I waited. Waiting for your letters was the only thing that kept me going. Then they never came."

"I'm sorry."

"Is that all you can say? I'm sorry? Like you bumped into me or belched or something? I was lonely, Jim. I was desperate. And then, well, there was this guy. At the lake."

"I thought so."

"Well, what of it? I mean, there I was stuck up there miles from anywhere—" She stopped and smiled to herself. "Miles," she said. "That was his name. Only I called him Milo."

Jim felt a surge of jealousy, but he pretended it

was anger. "So you screwed around with some clown named Miles, and now you don't want to with me, is that it?"

"We didn't 'screw around' as you put it. It wasn't like that at all."

"Oh? Just held hands on the shore of the lake? Built sand castles? That sort of thing?"

Mimi reached up and slapped his face. It startled him more than it hurt. "Shut up," she said. "Don't make fun of something when you don't understand it."

"Oh, I understand it all right. I can just see it. You sneaking off from camp—you told me you did that, remember? And there was this lake, and there was this guy. Oh, I can see it very clearly, Mimi baby. I know you well enough, don't forget, to know exactly what happened." He was wounding her on purpose, cutting deep with his words. He thought it was because he was jealous, but inside he felt there was another reason.

"Take me home, Jim."

"With pleasure."

They drove in silence back to town. He didn't look at Mimi, but he could hear her sniffling in the dark beside him. He felt awful. He'd been unkind—no, more than that. He had deliberately hurt her. That wasn't like him, he thought, to go out of his way to deliberately wound someone. Any more than it was like him to go out of his way to help someone, thinking of Gus Palmer.

"I'm sorry, Mimi," he said, his voice no more than a whisper. "I didn't mean to sound off like that. I don't know what made me do it."

She didn't answer at first, but she had stopped sniffling. Finally she said, "I guess it was my fault. I shouldn't have told you about Milo."

"Why did you, then?"

"I don't know. I guess maybe to make you jealous. Maybe that was part of it."

"And the rest?"

"What?"

"You said that was part of it. What's the rest?"

He glanced over at her. She was staring through the windshield, the tears still glistening on her cheek. She looked wistful, like a child. He wanted to take her in his arms again, but this time to protect her. She seemed so vulnerable.

"Maybe, somehow, I thought if I told you about Milo—Miles—it would go away. I'd forget about him, and we could go back to things the way they were. I want to, Jim. I don't want to hang in limbo like this."

"Where is he now—this Miles?"

"Oh, he's gone back to Ohio or Iowa or somewhere. To college. He was working at a logging camp up from where our camp was. For the summer. He was a senior in college."

"A senior in college?"

"I know. Too old. He was so—so different. I guess because of how old he was. That's what makes coming back so hard."

They had reached Mimi's house. Jim pulled up, turned off the ignition, then faced her. "So, where do we go from here?" he asked.

"I want to keep going together," she said. "Like I said, I want to forget Milo."

"You didn't do a very good job of it tonight."

She nodded. "I know. I'm sorry about that, Jim. Acting like that at Mandy's, and at the Gulley. I don't know, I just froze up. But it won't happen again. I think it's over."

"You *think* it's over? I'm supposed to get along on that?"

"You don't have to. You can do what you want." She started to open the car door, but he reached over and grabbed her arm.

"Tell you what, Mimi baby, let's forget tonight happened. We've both said things we shouldn't have. Let's erase it, pretend it didn't happen and go on from there."

She smiled. He liked the innocence in her eyes. She believed him, even though he was talking nonsense. "Can we, Jim? I'd like that."

"Why not? We're in control of time, Mimi. We can erase tonight—and while we're at it, let's do away with the whole summer. It didn't happen."

"Okay." She kissed him, her lips clinging to his. "It didn't happen." Then she opened the car door and got out.

Jim watched her as she went up the curving walk into her house. Once again he thought about the image of quicksilver. Or was it flashing water, falling over pebbles in a small stream? Beautiful Mimi, who believed anything was possible. Maybe she was right. Maybe pretending things didn't happen would make them go away.

9

On Wednesday Dundee perched on his desk and placed the themes on his knee. "It seems death means different things to different people."

Jim felt the blood pounding at his temples. Would Dundee suspect that someone else had written his theme? He tried to remember what it said, but he couldn't recall a word of it.

"Your papers gave me pause, as Hamlet might have said. Had he been an English teacher." A few students groaned good-naturedly. In just a few days Dundee had recaptured them with his combination of strict discipline and honest warmth. As he always did, Jim thought. But was any of it honest? Since the first day when Dundee's dramatizing had seemed so staged, Jim had wondered about that.

Dundee read the papers aloud, giving them the same dramatic rendition he did with literature. He paused occasionally to comment to the students who wrote them. "Marianne, yours is one of the best. Having a friend struck by lightning in the fifth grade must have been a devastating experience."

"Shocking, more likely," put in one of the boys, but Dundee frowned him into silence.

"But do more with it. The suddenness of such a death. The symbolism even. Know what I mean?"

The girl nodded.

"John, your story about your dog is a nice sentimental piece. I have no quarrel with it. It's honest. That's what I'm after here, class—honesty. Complete honesty." At that moment, his eyes fell on Jim, then darted away.

"Helen, your piece about funerals has promise. I have no doubt you really think they are barbarous. But I want you to give it more, well, guts. Not textbook funerals. Real reactions to a real funeral. Have you ever been to one?"

"A funeral? *Yuck.* No. And I hope I never do."

"But you should. If you're going to preach about them, you should attend one."

"Go to a funeral? Mr. Dundee—"

"Either that or a graveyard. In fact, class, that wouldn't be a bad idea for all of us. Perhaps a field trip. I'll try to arrange it."

"Are you serious, man?" Len put in. "Go to some poor cat's funeral as a field trip?"

"I meant a graveyard, Len. I think that would be best."

Dundee's talk of funerals had lulled Jim nearly

asleep. He was looking at the fish in the tank near his
desk when Dundee called his name.

"Halbert, what kind of crap is this?" He was holding out the paper Gus had written.

Jim sat up.

"Class, I saved this paper for last because it upset
me far more than any of the others."

The class had turned to look at Jim, but now they
gave their attention back to Dundee as he read from
the paper.

" 'Death means nothing to me. Because I plan to
live forever.' An interesting thought, class. And not an
uncommon one. Everyone feels that way. We can't accept the reality of our own death. I said to myself
when I started this paper, now, here is a boy who is
completely honest. But he let me down with a thud in
the second paragraph. I'll read it through."

As Dundee read, Jim remembered the words he'd
copied so hurriedly in study on Friday. It was like a
treatise on the future—an outline for a science-fiction
story. She'd talked about developments in science that
would make death obsolete—cloning, organ trans-
plants, cybernetics. It was clever, but it was not what
Dundee had wanted. He cursed Gus. Why couldn't
she have just written it straight? But then, he guessed,
Gus Palmer never did anything the usual way.

"I had hoped in this assignment to touch a nerve.
To dredge up from wherever it lurks, a monster. A

monster called Death. I wanted you to see it for what it is. Most of your papers were fishing in the right ponds, but you didn't go deep enough. That takes time, I guess, and that's what I'm here for. But at least you tried. All but you, Jim. You didn't even try.

"I ask for honesty and I get crap. Crap about cloning. Crap about freezing. Crap!" His voice rose with each repetition of the word.

"Hey, man, take it easy," Len said.

"All right, all right. I'm being hard on you, I guess. I want you to try—all of you—to reach deep into yourselves and find that truth about death. Your rewrites are due Friday."

Jim would not meet Dundee's eye. He looked instead at the fish, wishing he were one of them and Dundee's voice nothing but a meaningless roar. Dundee passed out the papers.

When he reached Jim's desk, he paused. "See me after class."

Jim waited until the room emptied of students, then stood up.

Dundee was coming down the aisle toward him. He didn't speak but stopped at the fish tank and sprinkled some powdered food on top. "I know what you must be thinking," he said. Jim thought at first he was addressing the fish. Then he turned. "You think I'm a monster. Prodding you kids like that in class. I saw how they looked at me."

Jim didn't say anything, just traced the deep grooves on his desk with a forefinger.

"There's a reason for what I'm doing, Jim. I think in time you'll come to understand it." He paused, waiting for a response. When none came, he cleared his throat and asked, "How's the team this year?"

The sudden shift of gears caught Jim off guard. "What?"

"The team? How's it look?"

"Okay. Well, actually, not too strong. We need a good fullback. Without Gardner, we're weak on the offense."

"What about you? You looked good last year."

"Yeah, well, we'll see."

"And your dad? Still coaching?"

"Sure."

"How do you feel about that, Jim?"

"I don't know. How should I feel?"

"Does it bother you? I mean, aren't you worried about him?"

"He's fine. He's doing just fine." Jim felt his ears burning.

"Shouldn't he be taking it easy? Riding it out?"

"Riding *what* out, sir?" Jim said each word carefully, so Dundee would hear the anger in his voice.

Dundee didn't answer, just looked at him.

Finally Jim said, "I have to get to lunch, Mr. Dundee. I'm meeting some friends."

"Of course. I didn't mean to keep you." He turned his attention to the fish once more, watching them fight for the food.

As Jim left, Dundee called him back. "Jim, I—" he stopped, then shook his head. "Nothing. Never mind."

10

As he was heading for the locker room after school, Jim heard his name called. He saw Gus Palmer, looking more disheveled than ever.

"I've got to catch the bus," she said, a little breathless, "but I wanted to tell you. I got an *A* on the math test."

"Well, you should," he quipped.

"Yeah, I know. I want to thank you—because you did it for me. Helping me and all. And Mr. Bowden praised me in front of the class. Said I'd made terrific progress in just a few days. Jesus, I never had that happen to me before. How'd I do on your English theme?"

"Uh, not so good. He could tell it wasn't mine."

"I tried to make it sound impersonal, like it could be anybody."

"I know. That was the trouble. He said it was too impersonal. Have to do it over."

"I could try again."

"No, that's all right. I guess I'd better tackle it myself this time." He felt a stinging at the roots of his hair. *How do you feel about your father still coaching?* Dundee had asked yesterday. Jim had not yet come up with an answer. Or rather he had not yet faced the real answer.

"Hell, there's the bus," Gus said.

Suddenly Jim realized he didn't want her to go. "Look, why not stay? I've got football practice, but if you want, we could drop by Mandy's and—uh— knock around some ideas for that theme. Maybe I'll get you to do it after all."

"That's the spirit. I feel real bad about lousing it up the first time. After everything you did for me. But I don't know diddlysquat about football."

"That's all right. Neither do I."

He led her to the door that opened out to the bleachers, then ducked into the locker room. The guys were changing, bantering with one another. The camaraderie of the locker room was one part of football Jim had always liked. Yet this year even that seemed hollow. The guys were friendly enough and tried to include him, but it was just that—they seemed to be working at it, making a point to include him instead of letting it come natural. And one thing he noticed in particular, when they were around him at least, they didn't call the coach any names. Not like they used to. He wondered if they had stopped that altogether.

He went to his locker and worked the combination. As he was suiting up, Len Wilson came over and clapped him on the shoulder.

"How's it going?" Len asked, as he always did.

"Okay, Len. What's the game plan today?"

"The first preseason scrimmage is set for next week. I guess Coach'll be riding us the whole time today. You know how he gets."

"Yeah." The talk was inane but comfortable, like a ritual.

Then Len's face changed. "I looked for you at lunch. I wanted to tell you what a creep I think Dundee is."

"Yeah? Well, he made me stay after. But all he did was feed the fish."

"He's some mean cat. He shouldn't be talking about death, not with you in the class. And hassling you the way he did today. What's with him, anyway?"

Jim reached into his locker for his jersey and slipped it over his head. "Who knows? But if it gives his little unit more pizazz to have a real live death to focus on, so much the better. In fact, maybe he could arrange to have one of us conk out right there in class. We could have a funeral too. No need for a field trip. Hands-on experience. What d'you say, man?"

"Cool it, Jim. Take it easy."

"What's the matter?" Bud Alden asked, coming up.

"We're going to have a funeral in English class, Bud. Want to come?"

"A funeral?" He turned to Len. "What's he talking about?"

"Nothing." Len put his hand on Jim's shoulder again. "Calm down, man. I'm sorry I said anything."

Jim blinked. "What? Hey, Len, I was just kidding. Fooling around."

"Yeah, I know. It's a bitch. And Dundee's making it worse."

Len squeezed his shoulder, but the feeling was muffled by the heavy pad. Ironic, Jim thought, that he should put on all this heavy padding to protect his body, but no padding on his most vulnerable part— that open wound deep inside that Dundee was probing.

"I don't get it," Bud said.

Len turned to him and led him away. "It's our English class, Bud. The creep's doing a unit on death."

"Death? You've got to be kidding. How can he? With Coach—"

Len hushed him, and they left by the swinging door that led to the field.

Jim slammed his locker door, clipped on the lock, and headed toward the field. It was then he remembered that Gus was out there waiting. His step lightened.

The sky hung heavy with clouds, threatening rain. A cold wind whipped at the flag near the goalpost at the far end of the field. Jim looked toward the bleachers. Gus was huddled at the top. The guys were standing around near the bench, reluctant to start their warmups before the coach came. Then Jim froze. Down from where the team was, a group of cheerleaders was rehearsing. There was no mistaking Mimi even in the subdued light of the cloudy day.

Jim glanced again at Gus, who waved. He smiled, then lifted his hand and made a tentative wave back. Mimi hadn't seen him yet, and he hoped she hadn't seen Gus.

His father came out, pushing past him and muttering, "Get on the field, boy. Time's a-wastin'." He called the team out and they began their warmups. Then Jake ordered them to the bench.

Mimi had seen Jim by that time and did an elaborate dance, her arms and legs akimbo. At the end of it, she gave him a thumbs-up sign and a winning smile. All was well, she was telling him. He managed a weak smile in return, the skin at the back of his neck tingling. He didn't look around, but of course Gus was still there. How long, he wondered, before Mimi saw her?

Jake began to pace back and forth, his hands folded

behind him. He was bent over at the waist, in the same position Jim had seen him shuffling down the hall, but here on the field, in front of the team, it looked like the strong stance of a tough coach. Jim marveled for a moment at how cleverly Jake turned his weaknesses into strengths.

"We have a scrimmage next week against Elmwood," Jake bellowed, spinning to face the team. "The first of the season. I know, you're all thinking it's only a preseason scrimmage that doesn't count. It counts. It counts a hell of a lot. It'll set the year off. It'll tell the whole state what sort of shape Woods Cross is in. And the whole state watches us—everything we do. The whole state waits for us to fall on our asses. And do you know what they're going to see next week?"

The boys squirmed, but they didn't reply. They knew Jake didn't want any answer.

"I think the whole state's gonna see us fall on our goddamned asses, that's what I think."

"Hell they will," shouted one of the boys in the back. The others turned their heads to gape at him. He was a sophomore, obviously new to the team. He didn't know you didn't answer the coach when he was giving his warmup speech.

Jake stepped back, startled. "Who the hell are you?" he asked.

The sophomore blushed and murmured his name.

"Well, let me tell you something, Francis—" then

he cocked his head to one side. "Francis? That really your name, boy?"

The sophomore gulped. "Yes, sir."

"On this team we don't have anyone called Francis. No Francises, no Melvins, no Marions. Get me?"

"I—I think so, sir."

"Call yourself Frank."

The boy nodded.

Jake added one last admonition: "And don't talk back to me."

The tone was gentle, though. Somehow the fear they'd always had of talking back to the coach was lessened by this exchange. Jim wondered if his father had indeed softened, or had no one ever made the mistake of answering before.

"But you're wrong, Frank, we are going to fall on our asses. On our own field next week. They're going to crush us under their cleats like we were bugs. And do you know why?"

He paused again. The boys were catching the spirit. Like a southern preacher, Jake milked his audience—pulling out the anger, the fear, using it. Like Dundee, Jim realized. Another ham actor.

It was strange to sit there noticing this for the first time. He'd sat through these sessions many times in the past two years. He remembered the season when they had one last game to cinch the pennant. Jake had

strode onto the field with a shoebox stuffed under his
arm. Like a magician pulling out rabbits, he'd opened
the lid of the box and pulled out a powder puff. It was
a large fluffy pink one. "See this?" Jake had hollered.
"Know what this is?"

The boys had nodded.

"There's eleven more of these here in this box."
Jake had upended the box and the puffs fell out like
thistles, floating to the ground. "Do you know where I
got them?"

No one knew.

"I got them in the mail. From Westview High.
This is what they think of Woods Cross. Of us. And
do you know what I think?"

The boys had not answered but had leaned forward, waiting.

"I think they're right!" He'd picked up the puffs
and had tossed them one at a time at the boys, who
caught them by reflex.

Now Jim wondered where Jake had really gotten
those puffs. If he'd bought them himself. He hadn't
thought about it at the time.

Jake had no powder puffs today, but his voice was
as firm as ever.

Fired up by their "quarrel" with the coach, the
team sped onto the field and began tossing the ball.
Jake put them into position, and they began.

It didn't go well. In spite of Jake's speech, or

maybe because of it, the boys fumbled, tripped, missed tackles, and generally proved to themselves that Jake was not far from the truth.

Jim had his share of mistakes, but he was able to stay out of his father's line of vision. Bud Alden couldn't. He was trying too hard as usual and falling too hard. He missed the signals when he was at quarterback and fumbled the ball three times. When he didn't fumble, he lost ground and was dragged back.

Jake lit into him. Bud lowered his head and pawed the ground with his cleats like a restless bull. Jim wished he could do something to soften the blow— God knows Jim knew what Bud was going through— but it was all happening too far away.

"Get over to that goddamned bench," Jake bellowed, "and stay there until you remember how to play this game."

Bud went to the bench, his head still down. Jim raised his eyes to where Gus sat, looking like a frail crow in her dark jacket. And over to Mimi in her bright red cheerleader's sweater. A perfect triangle, Jim realized. His good friend, his girl and—and what? What was Gus to him, and why was she here, looking miserable in the cold wind?

Watching them, he wished he were over there too, off this field, away from his father's snarls and the huffing of his teammates. He wanted to be on the bench with Bud, or just watching with Gus. He

cursed himself for his weakness in not quitting the
team while he had the chance.

"Halbert, get your butt over here!" Jake again,
searing into his thoughts. Jim ran across the field.

"Let's see if your receiving is any better than it
used to be. Start running."

Jim ran toward the far goalpost, looking over his
shoulder for the moment when Jake threw the ball. He
ran like a chicken, gawky and frightened, and still the
ball didn't come. When he had nearly given up, decid-
ing Jake didn't intend to throw it at all, it came. He
saw it against the backdrop of the school, then it was
in the air, the only dark spot in a gray slate sky. It
grew larger as it hurtled toward him, eclipsing the sky,
until it hovered just over his head.

Time seemed to slow down. The ball hung in the
air, spinning. He could see the laces forming patterns
as it rotated. He had slowed down too, as if he were
underwater, his hands floating toward the ball. He felt
the pockmarks in the leather and saw his fingers
splayed across the ball's sides.

"Okay, throw it over here."

He heard the words, and his thoughts snapped to
attention. He raised the ball over his head for a
forward pass, but it was not as easy to throw as it had
been to catch in the stillness of the water-air. It fell far
short of where Jake was standing.

"Good God, boy, what kind of pantywaist toss was

that?" The voice wrenched the air. "Get over here, Halbert. Pick up that goddamned ball and throw it like a man."

Like a man. Jim thought about that phrase as he ran toward the ball. How often he had heard it—long before he was anything close to being a man. When he was a small boy trying to catch one of Jake's passes with his tiny hands, Jake would cry, "Come on, not like that. Like a man."

Jim picked up the ball and raised it once more high above his head. He held it steady, his gaze riveted on his father. There was no more water-air, no more dreamlike floating. There was only the pounding of blood at Jim's temples and the rush of breath into his lungs.

"Come on, come on, Halbert. We haven't got all day. Throw the goddamned ball."

Jim threw it. He put all the strength he had into that throw. A lifetime of being told to be a man and somehow never quite making it, rode on the leather of that ball, in the power of that pass.

The ball sped like a bullet across the space between them, hitting Jake full in the chest.

The air puffed out of Jake. He collapsed like a tent on the field.

The team surged toward him, forming a huddle around his fallen body. Jim stood mute a few feet away, his arm still thrust forward. He remained there, paralyzed like one of those golden players on top of Jake's trophies.

"God, we'd better call an ambulance," someone next to him said. He brought his arm down slowly and turned.

"What?"

It was Len. He wasn't speaking to Jim, though his dark eyes searched Jim's face. "He isn't getting up this time. Hey, guys, get back. Give him some air. Somebody go in the building and call the hospital."

"I will," Jim volunteered and jogged toward the building before anyone could stop him.

Bud ran up to him. "What happened? Did he fall again?"

Jim only grunted and went on.

He saw Mimi standing on the track, and Gus coming down the bleachers. He tried to avoid them, but Mimi raced toward him.

"Jim, what's the matter? What happened?"

"Dad—uh—fell. Tripped on something, I guess. He's always saying the field is like a turnip patch."

Mimi grabbed his arm. "But is he all right? Why are the guys standing there? Why doesn't he get up?"

Jim tried to pull away, but before he could make any move, Gus was down from the bleachers.

"Jim, what happened? Is he all right?"

Mimi turned and took in Gus with a long gaze from head to toe. Her expression of concern changed.

Her face became hard. "What's *she* doing here?" she demanded.

Gus afforded her little more than a glance, then turned to Jim again. "I saw the whole thing. The ball came at him, and he went down. Like one of those straw figures guys use to practice with."

"I've got to call an ambulance," Jim muttered, moving away as nonchalantly as he could.

"No," Gus said. "I'll go. You go back over there to him."

"You can't, Gus," he said. "The phone's in the boys' locker room."

She shrugged. "Won't see anything I haven't seen before. Besides, everybody's out of there, aren't they?"

"Probably. No, I'd better go." He glanced back to where the boys were still standing. Someone had found a coat and covered Jake. Jim started away again, but he felt hands tugging at his arm.

"I asked you a question," Mimi said, her voice desperate.

"What?"

"I asked what she's doing here. Is she with you, or what?"

"It doesn't matter now, Mimi. Look, I've got to—"

"It matters to me," she said. "Because you said there wasn't anything going on. That you were just helping her with her math. I suppose that's what you were doing tonight, too. Just helping her with her—"

"Mimi, we'll have to talk about this later. My dad's unconscious out there, for Christ's sake." He pulled away and headed toward the locker room.

The phone was in the coach's office. He picked up the receiver, then stood there dumbly, trying to think.

"What's the matter?" It was Gus, standing in the doorway.

"It's silly, but I don't know how to call an ambulance. I never have before."

"Dial *0* and have them connect you. Or is there a '911' number in this town?"

" '911?' Yes, I think so."

"Here, let me." She took the receiver from him, dialed, and began to speak.

Jim sat down in the swivel chair, suddenly exhausted. He tuned out everything for a moment, then he felt a hand on his shoulder.

"They'll be over right away," Gus said.

"What? Oh, yes." He ran the sleeve of his jersey over his forehead, surprised that it was wet. He must have been sweating a lot. "Thanks, Gus."

"No problem. Look, I'll go back out and see if everything's okay. You stay here awhile. You probably need some time alone. I'll let you know when the ambulance gets here."

He nodded. After she'd gone he leaned back and closed his eyes, his hands gripping the arms of the chair. He let the thoughts he'd been trying to hide wash over him.

He saw himself as he must have looked out on the field. The team had been scattered. Not too many of the guys were near when it happened. Len must have been there because he appeared so suddenly at Jim's side. But from where they stood, could any of them have seen how Jim threw the ball, how hard, and how deliberately?

Gus had said she saw the whole thing. What did she mean? Had she seen him level the ball at his father and throw it hard enough to knock him down?

He opened his eyes and looked around the small, glass-enclosed room. Jake's desk was littered with papers, a rollbook already looking worn, and one of his many whistles. In a frame near the window was a picture of Liz, a younger Liz looking childlike because she seemed to have grown up so fast, and one of him—his team yearbook picture from last year. Jim was struck by the resemblance between that picture and the portrait down in the game room. They might have been the same person.

He heard the scream of a siren and roused himself. He was nearly out the door when Gus came to get him.

The field was in darkness except for the spotlights on the corners of the building. How quickly night comes, Jim thought. As he and Gus crossed the track, the ambulance came squealing into the driveway, its lights flashing a red arc across the milling boys. Two men in white climbed out of the back with a stretcher.

"Stand back, fellas. Let us in."

They were young, Jim noticed, not much older than high school boys. The thought flitted across his mind that they probably knew his father, maybe had been on the team once. They leaned over and examined him, their faces in the arc of light showing only impersonal concern.

Gus slipped her hands around Jim's upper arm and squeezed. "He'll be okay," she said. "He opened his eyes for a moment."

"He did?"

"Yeah. His eyelids fluttered for just a minute. Didn't you see?"

Jim shook his head. He looked down at his father's face as he lay on the stretcher. His eyes were closed, his skin ashen. "God," he muttered to himself, "what have I done?"

Gus heard him. "You didn't do anything," she said. "You threw the ball—a football. A football can't do that, knock a guy out, unless—" she paused. "I guess he's a lot weaker than he looks. I mean, the cancer. . . . " Her voice trailed off.

So she knew about that, he thought. But then, of course she would. Everyone at Woods Cross did. What made him think Gus wouldn't?

"Okay, clear the way, guys," the young men said, making their way with the stretcher through the crowd. "You fellas go on home. See that someone calls his family, will you?"

Jim stepped forward. "I—I'm his son."

It seemed to Jim that the impersonal concern left the young man's face, but then the light crossed it and he could no longer see his expression. "Okay, come along."

Jim climbed in the front seat of the ambulance next to the driver. The other young man stayed in the back with Jake.

Gus stood at the window for a moment, watching him. "I'll go over with the guys," she said. "I'll see you there."

Jim nodded. As he rode through the dark streets, the siren splitting the quiet, he thought about Gus— the concern on her face, her eyes resting on his, the way she had of knowing just what he needed—to be alone in the coach's office, to be alone now, and yet to have her there if he needed her. Then he thought of Mimi.

He hadn't seen her when he'd come out of the building, hadn't, in fact, even thought about her. She'd been so angry, and what about? Because Gus was there. Because he'd asked Gus to stay and watch practice. Mimi had a right to be angry, he guessed, if she thought it was a date he'd made with Gus. It

wasn't, of course, but he supposed Mimi could misin-
terpret it, the way she did in Mandy's that night. But
at that moment, with his father unconscious on the
field, why was *that* the only thing Mimi could think
about? He shook his head. He was never going to understand that girl.

11

They carried Jake through the emergency entrance, a lump on a stretcher, covered with a blanket. Paperwork and questions followed. Jim asked to use the phone.

His mother answered on the first ring. "Oh, Jim, I was getting worried. It's so late and—"

"Dad's in the county hospital, Mom."

She gasped. "I'll be there as fast as I can. Is he—how is he, Jim? Did you talk to him?"

"No." Was Jake conscious? Was he *alive?* Jim realized he didn't know. He hadn't hung around long enough to find out, had run off to the building to call the ambulance. To get away, really, as fast as he could. To run from what he'd done. "His eyes opened for a moment." Gus had seen it. It must have been so.

When Jim came back to the waiting room, he saw that Gus was there, flanked on either side by Len and Bud, both still in their blue and white jerseys. Bud's face was blotched and his eyelids swollen, Len's face solemn.

"How is he?" Len asked.

"They haven't come out yet," Jim answered. "They took him in there and they haven't come out yet."

Jim settled in a chair against the wall and stretched out his feet. A middle-aged couple came in, glanced at them, looked again, then went to the desk. They spoke in whispers to the nurse, glancing back over their shoulders at them.

Len began to chuckle. It was a strange sound in the hushed room, the low velvet chuckle that started deep in his throat.

"What the hell?" Bud asked.

"Sorry, man," Len said. "I just realized how we must look. Three big hulks in football jerseys, covered with mud. It struck me funny."

"I don't see the joke," Bud said sourly.

"Sorry." Len became serious at once and dropped his gaze to stare at the floor between his dangling hands.

"Jesus, I wish they'd come out. Say something."

"How—how was he," Jim ventured, "after I left? Did he try to get up or anything?"

"No. He was out for the count."

"He—he just laid there. Didn't open his eyes, nothing," Bud put in.

"He was breathing, though," Len said. "When I spread the blanket over him, I put my ear down by his mouth. I could feel his breath."

"He shouldn't have been out there," Bud said fervently, "running around the field like that. He could have coached from the sidelines the way Griswold does. He didn't have to be out there."

The outside door opened, and Jim's mother came in with Liz at her heels. They came like a wind sweeping through the door, his mother glancing quickly at the boys and then going to the desk.

Liz came over to them. "What happened, Jim? Did he fall again?"

Before Jim could answer, the swinging door opened, and a doctor came out. "Mrs. Halbert?"

"Oh, yes, Dr. Bartlett. Thank God you're here."

"I was on duty tonight."

"How is he? Is he—"

"Stable. But we want to keep him for a few days. We'll have him checked into a room."

"May I see him?"

"In a while. After he's settled in."

The door opened again, and Jake was wheeled out on a stretcher. This time his eyes were open. Jim's mother went to him.

For a moment Jim hesitated, but Gus's eyes were searching his. *Go to him*, they said. Bud was already on his feet, but Len put out a hand and held him back.

Jake's eyes were bloodshot, his expression impossible to read. His lips were moving, but no sound came out. Jim's mother held his hand and was trying to talk to him.

Dr. Bartlett put his arm around her. "Not just yet," he said gently. "He's had a shot. When he's settled, we'll call you." He led her away.

Liz stood uncertainly in the hallway, watching as they wheeled Jake away. "Daddy?" she said, but no one paid any attention to her.

Dr. Bartlett looked at the group. "Happen during a game?" he asked.

"Practice," Bud told him. "He was out on the field and then suddenly—I don't know, he fell. Is he going to be all right?"

"Hard to tell. But at least he's conscious." He put his hand on Jim's arm, clutching the thick shoulder pad. "Look, fellas, there isn't much you can do tonight. You might as well go on home." He turned and went down the hall.

Len stood up. "Look, Bud, we might as well head out. We're just taking up space here. Jim'll let us know how he is."

Bud hesitated. He'd heard the doctor say the same thing, but Jim wasn't leaving. Jim was family.

"I'll give you a call, Bud," Jim assured him. "As soon as I've seen him."

Still Bud didn't move. The nurse behind her desk

was looking at them askance. These great hulks in their garish uniforms covered with grime, why didn't they leave? They were so out of place in the muted colors of the waiting room.

Jim gripped Bud's arm. "He'll be fine, Bud. You heard what the doctor said."

Bud nodded, and Jim saw the tears standing in his eyes.

Gus stood up and slipped her bag over her shoulder. "Either of you guys live near West Avenue?" she asked.

"Just down the street from there," Len said. "Come on, let's get out of here."

Gus went over to Jim and took his hand. "I'll just go on with these guys," she said. "But if you get a chance, let me know how he is." She grinned. "I mean, I want to know if I have to dig up that goddamned gym suit or whether I'm off the hook, you know?" She turned, then turned back. "Oh, by the way, I've got a message for you. From that blond dame."

"Oh?"

"Yeah. She said if you don't call her tonight, don't call her again. She said you'd understand."

After they'd gone the room seemed larger. The two people who'd come in earlier were eyeing them. Jim sat beside his mother. Liz was on the other side holding her mother's hand tightly in her own.

"This is it, Jim," his mother said. "I'm not going to have it anymore."

"Have what, Mom?"

"This football business. This is the second time in less than a week. He can't handle it. I won't have it."

"Mom, Dad's going to coach as long as he can. You know that."

"And kill himself inside a month? Because that's what's going to happen, Jim. We'll be sitting here again, only there won't be any hope that time. They'll come out and say he's gone. I'm almost afraid that's going to happen this time." She brought a wad of Kleenex to her nose and sniffed. Her eyes were watery, but no tears flowed. "There's got to be somebody else. Another coach."

"There's Griswold. He coaches the freshmen."

"Then Coach Griswold is going to do it," his mother said with such a tone of finality there was no questioning it.

Dr. Bartlett came back. "He's settled now. But only stay a few moments. He needs rest."

Jim and Liz waited outside the door while their mother went in.

Liz looked at him, her eyes serious. "Do you think he'll do it, Jim? Quit coaching?"

"Are you kidding, Liz? Dad give up coaching?"

She nodded. "That's what I thought. But Mom seems so sure. I mean, he keeps collapsing. I mean, it was only last Thursday when it happened before."

Jim licked his lips, forming the words in the hushed hallway. "This time he didn't just collapse. He—he was hit by a ball." Still he left himself out, left the ball disembodied, attacking on its own.

"Hit by a ball? A football?" she asked.

The door opened, and their mother looked out. "Come in now. He wants to see you."

They crept into the room. A light on the bedside table poured across Jake's face, but otherwise the room was in darkness. Jake lay propped up on a pillow. In the dim light his face looked ashen, but his eyes glittered under his half-closed lids. He looked straight at Jim.

Jim moved forward as if walking through molasses. Fear tightened in his chest. Liz was somewhere in the background and behind her, his mother, but it was Jim Jake stared at, drawing him forward until he was standing at the bedside.

He looks old, Jim thought. His face was ridged with deep crevices, like the gulleys running through the foothills outside of town. A drop of spittle gleamed on Jake's lower lip. His tongue darted out and caught it.

"*Hmmmoy.*"

Jim leaned closer, putting his ear nearly on Jake's cheek. He could hear the rasp of Jake's breathing and smell his sour sweat.

"What, Dad?"

"Hell—hell—" Jake licked his lips once more, took a deep breath, and said, "Hell of a pass, boy."

Jim spun his head and looked at his father, but Jake had closed his eyes and was smiling slightly. Jim stood up and let Liz take his place.

Liz leaned down and stared at her father, then turned to Jim. "He looks so—so still," she said.

Jim nodded, but he barely heard what she said. What did he mean, "Hell of a pass?" All his life he'd gotten nothing but criticism from Jake. He could do nothing right. Now, when he threw the ball with all the fury he'd built up through the years, he'd heard, "Hell of a pass, boy."

"Shit!" Jim interrupted something Liz was saying, turned, and left the room. He walked down the hallway, the band of lights overhead pulling him on. One thought soared through his head. If Jake went back to coaching, he'd quit the team for certain. He'd never go back on that field as long as his father was there. He never wanted to feel that angry again, angry enough to kill. And he never wanted to feel as humiliated as he felt now.

In the middle of the night he woke up and realized he hadn't called Mimi.

12

All that week Mimi avoided Jim in study hall, leaving quickly before he could speak to her. He wasn't sure he was going to, anyway, and besides, he was sitting with Gus. He knew he'd have to sort things out with Mimi eventually, but right now he had all he could handle with his father in the hospital.

And with Dundee. The unit on death continued relentlessly.

Today Dundee came to class with a sheaf of xeroxed papers and began handing them out. "We have some poems to read—about death. Death is a popular subject for poets. Why do you suppose that is?"

He elicited a few responses. Jim glanced at the first poem. "To an Athlete Dying Young." He felt the knot tighten in his stomach again. *He doesn't give up, does he?*

"This poem takes a different view of death," Dundee was saying. "It almost seems to praise death. See what you think." He began to read.

> "The time you won your town the race,
>   We chaired you through the marketplace;
>   Man and boy stood cheering by,
>   And home we brought you shoulder-high,
>   Today the road all runners come
>   Shoulder-high we bring you home,
>   And set you at your threshold down,
>   Townsman of a stiller town."

He paused. The room was quiet. Jim's eyes drifted to the fish tank. He noticed one of the fish was floating on top of the water. He looked back at Dundee, the thought of the dead fish floating on the surface of his mind.

> "Now you will not swell the rout
>   Of lads that wore their honors out.
>   Runners whom renown outran
>   And the name died before the man."

Dundee paused again, took a breath, and looked straight at Jim.

> "So set before its echoes fade,
>   The fleet foot on the sill of shade,

And hold to the low lintel up
The still-defended challenge-cup."

Dundee's eyes searched the room. "Let's see what the poet is getting at," he said, all teacher again. "Melissa, why is it good that the athlete died young?"

Melissa, who'd been combing her hair during the reading, looked startled. "Good?" she gulped.

"Yes. The poet praises him for dying young. Why?"

"I don't think it's good to die young."

"I didn't ask you what you thought, Melissa. I asked you what the poet said."

Dundee was edgy today, Jim thought. Not like him.

"Brad?" Dundee pointed to another student.

"He says it's good because then the guy won't outlive his glory. He'll be remembered as a hero."

"Yeah," put in Len, "like Muhammad Ali."

"But he isn't dead, Len."

"I know. And he's turning into a slob. He ought to stay retired, at least."

"I don't follow. What's that got to do with the poem?"

"Like the guy says. Because the dude dies young, he doesn't turn into a slob. He's remembered as the athlete who won the race. If he went on living, he'd be like Ali—getting fat and foolish. He ought to retire."

"Well," Dundee said testily. "At least you're not recommending that he die."

Once again Jim was aware of a difference in Dundee's voice. He was not sympathetic to the students. What was bugging him, anyway?

"I think that's awful!" a girl in front of Jim said. Heads turned.

The girl blushed, embarrassed that she had spoken so loudly. "I mean, I agree that's what the poet meant, but I don't agree that the guy—the athlete—should die young. I think that's stupid."

"Why is it the only word you kids know is stupid? A new idea is always dubbed stupid—it's like a tradition. Oh, and boring. Yes, I forgot your other word, boring. Things are either stupid or boring."

The girl sank back in her chair, her face bright red.

"Hey, man," Len put in, "are you saying it's good to die young?"

"Weren't you, Len?"

"No, man, I wasn't saying that at all. I was saying that's what the poet said. I wasn't agreeing with him. No way."

Dundee stared at him for a long time. Then he said, "Let's read the other poem."

As Dundee read, Jim's mind wandered. He thought about one night last summer when his mother had come into his room to talk to him. He'd been painting all day and had flung himself across his bed, dog tired and smelling of turpentine.

His mother sat timidly in his desk chair, facing him, and spoke more to her whitened knuckles than to him.

"Mr. Weaver stopped by today," she began, and for a moment Jim was confused. What could the school principal want with him during the summer? "He wants to set up a memorial fund—a scholarship in your father's name. For promising athletes."

"What did you tell him?"

"I don't think it would be a good idea this year. Maybe next year. After—after—" She lowered her head.

Jim wished he knew how to comfort her.

She recovered herself, then looked up, her eyes no longer watery. "Your father is a hero in this town. He'll always be remembered that way. That's why I don't think a memorial fund is a good idea this year. It will call attention to his—his dying. I don't want that. I wish. . . ."

"Wish what, Mom?"

"I wish he wouldn't go back this year. Then he'd be remembered as he was."

Jim caught the last part of Dundee's reading. He looked up in time to realize, with a shock, that

Dundee was weeping. He put down the xeroxed sheet, which missed the edge of the desk and fluttered to the floor.

"Class," Dundee said, "I want to tell you a story. I didn't want my own feelings to intrude on this unit; I wanted to remain objective. But last night when I was going over these poems, I remembered something. I thought about my father. When I was nine years old he hanged himself from a Ferris wheel in an amusement park."

Someone gasped. Jim sat up and looked at Mr. Dundee.

"I was at school when it happened. The principal called me to his office and told me. It was just one of the chores he had to do that day—sandwiched in between bus duty and supervising the lunchroom. He told me and then left me alone in his office to wait for someone to take me home.

"I sat there on this hard wooden chair—I can still feel it—staring at an aquarium he had behind his desk. I just watched those fish swimming back and forth— mindless fish who didn't have to think about such things as death." He paused. His hand, which had been swimming in the air, stopped, thrust out toward the class. He had them fully into his story.

Jim felt his temper rising once again. What was Dundee up to now? He'd do anything to get the right effect.

"And suddenly I was angry—no, not angry, I was furious. I hated those fish as I don't think I'll ever hate anything again. I hated their mindlessness, their freedom. They had nothing to worry about except swimming around their make-believe plaster castle. I grabbed the handiest thing—it turned out to be a stone ashtray on the desk—and threw it as hard as I could at the tank. The glass shattered, and water and fish came pouring out onto the carpet. The fish flapped around, their mouths gaping." His eyes traveled to the fish tank near Jim's desk. "My God, there's a dead fish in there," he said.

The anger that had been seething just below the surface erupted. Jim stood up, clenching his fists at his sides. "You knew that all the time, didn't you?"

"What?"

"You knew there was a dead fish in there. You probably made up your whole story just to lead up to the magic moment of discovering that dead fish."

"Sit down, Jim," Dundee said it gently, but there was an edge to his voice.

Jim addressed the class. "He's making fools of us, guys, do you know that? His father's probably living somewhere in Paterson, New Jersey, and never went near a Ferris wheel in his life. And"—he turned once more to Dundee—"there was never any sea gull in Bermuda either, was there?"

"Jim, I said sit down."

"There's only one death around here that's real, and that's the one he's very careful not to mention. Oh, but it's there, it hangs in the air every day, just waiting for the right dramatic moment when Dundee will produce it like a rabbit out of a hat."

Dundee took a step toward Jim, his hand out. Jim couldn't tell whether Dundee intended to strike him or take his hand. "Jim, calm down," Dundee said.

"I'll do better than that. I'm getting out of here right now, and I'm not coming back. You and your goddamned Ferris wheel and your fish. What the hell do you really know about death? You don't have any idea what it's like!"

As Jim headed toward the door, the bell rang. He walked blindly through the halls, melting into the crowd.

13

Jim started toward the lunchroom, then stopped. After his outburst in English class, he didn't feel he could face anyone who might be there. He wasn't hungry, either.

He stepped out of the mainstream of passing students into a recess in the wall between the lockers. He wished he were invisible. Earlier he'd hated the fact that no one looked at him, but now he wished he couldn't be seen. He thought about the class, wondering what had made him do that. He'd been sitting there, half listening to Dundee's voice, and suddenly he had lost all control, just as he had on the football field. What was happening to him?

Suddenly he wanted to see his father. He didn't know why, but he did.

He started toward the office to get a pass to leave school, but when he passed the Guidance Office, he heard his name called. Gus Palmer was in the middle of a crowd of milling students.

"Hey, Halbert, come and rescue me. I've been carried away by orcs, and they're turning me into a shadow of my former self."

He laughed and stepped into the doorway. "What's the problem?"

"I got in a fight. With these girls here. They were giving me grief, so I punched one of them out. So, instead of fighting back, they come bellyaching in here, but now nobody will see us."

The door to the counselor's office opened, and Mr. Amadeo came out. The girls streamed forward.

"Mr. Amadeo, this—this girl attacked me. Right in the cafeteria. And Mr. McNeil threw us all out. But it wasn't our fault."

Mr. Amadeo ushered them in, motioned for Gus to wait, and closed the door.

"This is going to take forever," Gus said. "Let's blow the joint."

"But, can you? I mean, won't he call you in next?"

"If he wants me, he can have me paged."

They went together down the hall.

"So, what are you up to?" She glanced at his hand. "What, no hall pass? Are you daring to walk these hallowed halls without a pass?"

Jim took in her mocking grin. "I'm leaving the building for a while."

"But not without a pass. I know, you're on the way to get one."

He nearly said yes, but something in the way she

was teasing him made him stop. "Nope. Just going. Over the hill. AWOL."

She whistled. "Geez, what's the world coming to? Where you headed?"

"The hospital. To see my dad."

"You could get a pass for that, couldn't you?"

"Probably. But what's the point? Following the rules around here gets you nowhere."

"Yeah, I can appreciate that."

"You can?" His voice was raw. Some of the rage he'd felt in the classroom was returning. "How can you appreciate that? What do you know about it, anyway?"

"Hey, this is me—Gus. I'm on your side."

"I'm sorry. I'm just jumpy today, I guess."

"You sure are. Hey, look, you want a tag-a-long?"

"A tag-a-long?"

"Yeah. A shadow. If you want, I'll go with you. Not go in or anything, but hang around outside. You act like you need somebody today. If only just to kick around."

He laughed and slipped his arm around her bony shoulders. "What about class? What about Mr. Amadeo?"

"Screw Mr. Amadeo. I'm already in so much deep water, a few more inches can't hurt. They're talking about suspending me. So I'll suspend myself."

"I don't want to get you in trouble, Gus."

"Trouble I can get myself into without any help. But if you don't want me to go with you, just say so and I'll buzz off. No hard feelings."

He thought about it. "I do want you, Gus. I—I need to talk some things out. But I'm in a rotten mood today. I blew up in English and told the teacher to go fuck himself."

"Not in those exact words, I'll wager."

"No."

"See, Halbert, you need me. You do things half-assed. Hang around with me long enough, and you'll learn to do 'em proper."

They left the building laughing. It was a beautiful day, one of those fall days that could just as easily be early spring. Jim started the car and drove out of the parking lot, feeling suddenly free.

"Don't they patrol out here too?" Gus asked.

"Sometimes. If they stop us, I'll just tell them who I am. Being the son of the coach has its advantages." His tone was bitter.

Gus put her hand on his arm. "Hey, take it easy."

Jim turned to look at her, at that face that just missed being pretty and became instead a comic face, a joke, with its pointed chin and too-wide mouth. But it was a face you could trust, maybe even love. "Thanks, Gus. I needed that. But I shouldn't lay it on you. I'm carrying around a lot of hate and guilt and crap. You don't need to get mixed up in it."

She shrugged her shoulders. "I may be skinny, but I'm strong as a mule, Jim. Besides, the burden is only heavy to you. I'm a disinterested third party. Only not so disinterested."

He headed toward the highway.

"How is your dad?"

"Better. They'll probably let him come home in a few days. Mom says he's mean as a bear with a sore head."

"Yeah. From what I hear, he can be. That's a good sign."

"I guess." He drove fast, reaching the highway sooner than he expected. Just before he went up the ramp, he pulled off. "Jesus, Gus, what am I doing? I don't want to go there."

"You don't?"

"No. Jesus. I was in the hall and suddenly I wanted to see him. I don't even know why. I'll see him tonight, anyway. I suppose I'll have to."

They sat in the car by the side of the road. Cars whizzed past them up the ramp.

"There's a pile of difference between wanting to and having to," Gus said.

"I know. I wanted to. There for a split second I really did."

"Why?"

"Christ, I don't know."

"Try to remember. It's important."

"Why? Why is it important?"

"Because if you wanted to see him, then you ought to know why. Because there's going to come some times when you'll want to see him, and you won't be able to."

Her words stung the air, seemed to still even the traffic above them on the highway. They hung between them. God, why did I bring her along? She's like my conscience.

"What were you thinking about?" she asked. "When you got this feeling you wanted to see him?"

"What difference does it make now?"

"Come on, Jim."

"I was thinking about Dundee. Goddamned Dundee and his fish. He's my English teacher. He'd been going on about his father's suicide, said he hung himself from a Ferris wheel, and suddenly I was so mad I walked out."

"Oh, I remember him. He's the one I wrote the paper for. He's big on death, right?"

"Exactly. Death is in style right now."

"And you were mad. Then what?"

"Then I remembered that night—on the field. When my father—I mean, when I threw that football at my father."

"You threw—"

"Yes, I threw it. I threw it hard. I threw it so hard I knocked him down. Knowing how weak he is, knowing he's dying, I threw a football with all my might. So, now do you want to go with me?"

"Hey, easy, easy. Man, you are carrying a load."

"Yeah. Come on, let's go back to school. This is stupid."

"Go see your father."

"What for? To get on my knees and ask forgiveness?"

"If you want to."

"I don't want to. I'm not sorry. He had it coming."

"So don't then. But go see him."

"What's the point? They probably won't even let me in. There aren't visiting hours, they'll say, or some damned thing."

"Probably not. When my dad was in the hospital down in West Virginia, I mean, when he got that black lung thing and had to have that operation, man, they treated us like shit. Like we were no better than so much garbage. All starch and whiteness and pursed lips. Visiting hours the first Tuesday of next year if there was a full moon."

"Your dad was a miner?"

"Yeah, all his life. Until the mines took their revenge. Now he works for a buddy of his who owns a gas station. That's why we came up here. There wasn't any work down where we come from."

Jim looked at Gus's tie-dyed shirt—the same shirt he'd seen her wear every day. And jeans. She probably didn't own any other clothes. But they were clean, and she wore them with pride. God, he thought, and I sit around feeling sorry for myself.

"Is he okay now? Your dad?"

"Sure. He's got one lung. Whoever put us together was smart that way—gave us two of most everything. Except our hearts. And our heads. Well, let's get a move on. I didn't cut out of that school to sit by the highway and jaw. Make up your mind what you want to do."

Jim started the car, then backed it out. Finally thrusting the gears, he headed up the ramp. "Bitch," he said.

Gus laughed.

The hospital looked different during the day. It was a squat red brick building on a patch of dried grass with a few scrawny trees around it. There was none of the drama of nighttime, with the ambulance flashing its arc of red.

"You coming?" he asked.

"I'll go in with you if you want. But I'll stay in the waiting room. There was a good story I got to the middle of the other night. Maybe I can finish it."

As they walked into the building, Jim felt her hand dangling near his. He clasped it, gently at first, then more strongly. She didn't seem to mind. He asked at the desk about visiting hours and found they lasted until two o'clock.

"I'll go over there and find that story. Take your time."

"I won't be long."

She gave his hand a squeeze as she let go of it. "Be long," she said quietly, looking steadily into his eyes.

He stood for a long time outside his father's door, looking at the gold-painted number, the squiggle of the *2*, the loop of the *3*, as if he would have to trace them. Finally he pushed the door open and went in.

The room was empty, the bed rumpled.

On the nightstand was a half-empty glass containing some brown liquid and a bent glass straw protruding from it.

I could leave, Jim thought. I could wander around the halls for a while, then tell Gus I saw him. I don't have to be here. He turned to go, but the door opened behind him.

"Oh, sorry." A nurse, half a head shorter than he and about as wide as she was tall, smiled at him. "Are you looking for Mr. Halbert?"

It seemed strange to hear him called "Mister." Always it was Coach, as if Jake had long ago shed the title "Mister" and exalted himself to a higher level. "Uh, yes."

"Was he expecting you? He didn't say anything about visitors."

"No. It was just an impulse. I—I don't need to see him. I'll come back tonight."

"You're his son, aren't you?" she asked.

"Yes."

"I thought so. You look like him. I mean, like he used to look. I went to high school with him. You wouldn't believe it now, but I was a cheerleader. And was he ever something. When he was on that field, he was beautiful. Like a god. You play football?"

"Uh, yes. A little."

"Of course, you would. Look, I wheeled him into the solarium a while back. You'll find him there."

"Wheeled?"

"Yes." She didn't say any more, but she wouldn't meet his eye. "I'll show you where it is. Then I'll just get this room made up."

He followed her out into the hall.

"Mr. Halbert's doing very well," she said. "Threw his breakfast at the orderly this morning."

"Threw his breakfast?"

"Yes. Said he was tired of the food. Well, he didn't say it exactly that way, but I'd rather not repeat what he said. I was across the hall taking temperatures, but I heard him. It's always a good sign when a patient begins to complain about the food."

"But you said 'wheeled.' A minute ago, you said you wheeled him to the solarium."

"Well, he's not too steady on his feet. But he's

okay. Can walk short distances. But as you see, it's a long way down here."

They'd reached the end of the hall. She pushed a swinging door, and they entered a small, sunny room. After the starkness of the hallway with its bank of fluorescent lights along the ceiling, the room was unexpectedly cheerful. There were plants everywhere—rubber plants stretching to the ceiling, swaying fronds of ferns, hanging ivy, spider plants with tiny versions of themselves at the ends of their thin leaves.

Patients in wheelchairs or settled in lounge chairs were chatting quietly; a couple of men were playing cards in the corner. A television set blared—ironically it was "General Hospital"—but nobody was watching. The blip of a Ping-Pong ball could be heard from another room.

"Your father was over by the window. At least that's where I left him earlier." She looked at the window in puzzlement. No one was there. She seemed disturbed by that. He wasn't where she left him. She plucked at her starched dress for a moment, uneasy about leaving Jim in the solarium alone, but finally, glancing at her watch, she sighed. "Maybe he went to look at the Ping-Pong table or something."

"I'll find him," Jim reassured her.

She smiled uneasily, glanced at her watch once more, and left.

Jim went over to the window and looked out. The

room overlooked the parking lot. He could see his Volkswagen parked slightly crooked. A black car pulled in beside it. A man in a gray suit carrying a doctor's bag climbed out. Unmistakable, he thought, the look of a doctor. Even without the bag he would have known.

He turned and let his eyes wander around the room. He didn't see Jake anywhere. Then he noticed an abandoned wheelchair near a side door.

The door led down a short hallway to a bathroom. Jim pushed open the bathroom door and looked in. There seemed to be no one in the small gleaming room, but as Jim turned to leave, he heard a sigh.

It might have been the creaking of the pipes or the rush of water through the network of hospital plumbing. Then he heard it again—not a sigh, but a sob.

Jim stood riveted to the spot, listening to the deep private sobs of a man sorrowing, or in pain. Then, under the booth, he saw the feet of a man, bare hairy legs thrust into battered slippers. Suddenly Jim recognized the slippers. His father shuffled about the house in those slippers, had worn them nearly threadbare, but wouldn't hear talk of any new ones.

The sobs finished in one great trumpeting of a nose blowing, and the toilet flushed. Jim was out the door in a flash.

He passed the wheelchair, affording it little more

than a glance, and hurried out of the solarium. He took the hallway at a jogtrot, putting as much distance as he could between himself and that sobbing man in the bathroom.

Not until he was leaning against the back rail of the elevator did he relax enough to think about what he'd done and why. He told himself he'd done it for his father's sake. He knew Jake wouldn't want him to witness that moment of weakness, of pain. But was that the real reason? Didn't he really run because he was afraid? Afraid of what his father would say seeing him there spying on him?

"That was quick," Gus commented when he joined her in the waiting room. "I thought you'd be a lot longer."

"Let's go."

"How's your dad?"

Jim thought about his father as he must have been, bent over in the booth, crying with agony. "He's fine. They told me he threw his breakfast at the orderly this morning."

She laughed. "Then he's getting better. My dad when he was in with his lung thing began to pull at his stitches. Said he felt like a crazy quilt and that Gram could stitch better than that and he was going up the mountain and have her do it proper."

"Will you cut the hillbilly act?"

"What?"

"Your dad and his black lung! I'm sick of hearing about it." The burst of anger seemed to take the air out of the room.

Gus turned white; her mouth dropped open. For once she had no quick comeback.

"Come on. Let's get out of here." He pulled her toward the door.

She let him lead her until they were outside, then she yanked her arm out of his grasp, swung her beaded bag up on her shoulder again, and walked swiftly toward the car. Meekly Jim followed, wondering how he could take back the words.

They drove in silence along the highway.

Finally, just before the turnoff, Jim said, "Gus. I'm sorry. I don't know why I did that."

He glanced over and saw tears in her eyes. She flipped her head, blinking quickly. Mimi, he thought, would have made the most of it, let the tears fill her large blue eyes, knowing they would wrench his heart. Funny, he thought, remembering the last time he'd been with Mimi in this car, she was crying too. I seem to be good at making girls cry, he thought. Then he remembered that other crying—the deep unmanly sob in the privacy of a toilet booth.

"I guess I do go on about him too much—my dad," Gus said. "I guess I had it coming. I mean, trying to compare my dad's thing with what's happening to your dad. But there was a time, Jim, when we didn't know if he'd make it. I mean, he had it bad, you know, and he'd had it for a long time. He wouldn't quit the old mine, and I used to hear him coughing in the night. Me and my sisters' room was right next to theirs, and Dad would cough most of the night. Course he knew if he let on, he'd be through at the mine. But finally he had to, there was no more hiding it. They took out the one lung, and he's alive. But sometimes I think he'd have been better off dying in that old mine."

"Why, Gus?"

"It broke him. When they took out that lung and made him quit the mine, hell, they took out his heart too. He just ain't the same anymore. Course having to live here in this hoity town, living above the cheese shop and pumping gas like a kid—oh, Jesus, there I go again. Shut me up, will you, Jim? Give me a slap on the mouth or something when I get going." She gazed out the window.

Jim wanted to reach out to her, to hold her close, to meld her pain with his own. When he left the highway, he didn't head back to town, but past the stubbled fields to the crack in the hills they called the Gulley.

14

Jim parked in front of the cheese shop, then turned. "Gus, I—"

She put her hand on his where it gripped the steering wheel. "No, don't go spoiling things by telling me you're sorry. Because I'm not, not a bit. You were uptight about what happened in the hospital, and you felt a little sorry for me."

"No, Gus, that isn't true. It wasn't like that at all."

"Don't worry about it. I know how I come across. Maybe I do it on purpose, I don't know. But, whatever the reason, it was great, Jim. I'm glad I was there on the receiving end. Receiving end. That sounds like football. Isn't that something in football?"

"Yes. And that's where I'd better be right now."

She got out of the car, but he called her back. "Gus, I'll call you. Soon, I promise."

She waved and hurried down the alley without looking back. He watched the shoppers passing along the sidewalk. Had he used her, the way she said? His passion, rising suddenly and unexpectedly, had refreshed and exhausted him. But now he was depressed.

He thought about Gus, how she'd been. As in everything, she was direct—no coyness, no bullshit. He'd kissed her long neck, the slightly protruding throat, her tiny pointed breasts through the cloth of her T-shirt. Then, pushing him aside, she'd pulled her shirt off. She was wearing no bra. He'd brought his lips to her nipples and then down the ribs that stuck out like xylophone keys. When finally he'd thrust himself into her, it was with a drive that verged on anger, not unlike, he thought now, the anger he'd felt when he threw the ball at his father.

How different making love to Gus was from making love to Mimi. Always with Mimi he'd have to be gentle, testing her every response, listening for her signs, before he went any further. Like crossing a wet floor, he thought.

But the thought of Mimi aroused him again. Mimi's soft flesh, Mimi's perfume. God, he thought, what the hell am I doing? Gus Palmer, for Christ's sake. Going to the Gulley with Gus Palmer, and leaving Mimi hanging. What the hell's the matter with me, anyway?

He'd call Mimi as soon as practice was over. Of if the cheerleaders were on the field today, he'd talk to

her. Make her understand somehow. Tell her he'd
gone off the deep end for a while, but he was all right
now.

He dressed quickly and hurried out to the field
where Coach Griswold was talking to the team. Jim
could hear his deep voice, so different from the high-
pitched squalling of his father. The guys hunched in
their uniforms. Jim slipped in beside Bud.

"Tomorrow is going to show," Griswold was saying. "If we can pull it off tomorrow, we can make it
through the season. Trouble is, you guys haven't
pulled it together yet. I've been watching you. You
play well, but you play separate. You're a team.
You've got to play like a team. What Woods Cross
needs is a team."

"What Woods Cross needs," muttered Bud under
his breath, "is a *coach.*"

"I know there's no star, no hotshot like Gardner
last year. Though, Halbert, you could be that good if
you put your mind to it."

Jim lowered his head as the eyes of his teammates
turned toward him.

"But, as a team, you guys need work. I've been
watching you, and you know how to work like a machine. Now let's get out on that field and try out some
of these strategies."

The boys got up from the bench, slipping on their
helmets.

Bud walked with Jim. "You're late. You missed his so-called strategies."

"I went out to the hospital."

"Oh? How's Coach?"

"Better. He threw his breakfast at an orderly." Is that all I can say? he asked himself bitterly, like a litany I recite whenever anyone pulls the string.

Bud laughed. "Hell, he's back to normal! When's he get out?"

"I don't know. Pretty soon, I guess."

Jim studied his friend, remembering the times they'd spent together—the night they slipped out and slept in the canyon. All they'd shared. Mostly they'd shared Jake. Could Jim share the truth with Bud? Could he say, Bud, he's in such pain. I don't know how to reach that pain.

"Bud—"

"Goddamn, I wish he could get back for tomorrow's game. We're going to be creamed. Work like a machine! Hell, we're like a lot of little bolts and nuts without the engine. The engine's gone."

"We're the same team, Bud. Same guys as before."

"No. Not without him. We're nothing without him." He pulled on his helmet and ran out across the field, joining the huddle.

As Jim crossed the field, Griswold clapped him on the shoulder. He was wearing his gray sweatsuit with *W.C. Athletic Department* stamped across the back.

Once during a game the opposing team had taken up the cry, "W.C., W.C., we know what a W.C. is used for and that's where you're gonna be!" Jake, hearing the chant, had turned red. He refused to wear his sweatshirt until they bought him a new one with "Woods Cross" stenciled on it. Somehow, thinking about that, Jim found he was laughing.

"How's the old man?" Griswold asked.

"Better. He threw—" He stopped. "Getting better. Up and about."

"Good news. Hell of a guy."

Jim searched his tone for irony, his face for a mask. There was none. Griswold meant it. Of course, it was only a matter of time, Jim thought, and Griswold would be the varsity coach. Jake always said Griswold was just waiting in the wings like some damned understudy. Yet, Jim wondered, watching Griswold run back across the field, his pale hair glinting in the fall sunlight, would taking the job be that easy? How do you take a hero's place, anyway?

Practice went well. As if to prove Griswold's point, the team worked together. Jim himself got back some of the old spirit he'd remembered as a freshman. He caught the ball when it was thrown and passed it smoothly with no heroics and no fumbles. If they'd been in a real game, they would have had a chance at winning.

Only Bud Alden seemed out of joint with the

smoothness of the football machine. He missed passes, stumbled and fell before he was tackled, mixed up signals, and went out of bounds before he had to. At length, Griswold put him on the bench where he sat like a blotch against the gray sky.

Jim showered next to Bud. When they were toweling themselves, Bud asked, "What are the chances of seeing the coach? At the hospital, I mean."

"I don't know, Bud. He didn't have visitors at first, just us. I don't know how it is now. Honest."

"I want to tell him to get the hell back here. Get his butt back here and coach this team." Bud smiled. It was a smile without joy, an attempt to laugh at his own imitation of Jake, which fell flat.

"It'll be a while, Bud, before he can do that. He— he's a lot weaker than he was."

Jim thought about his mother that first night when Jake went to the hospital, her fists clenched in her lap. "He's not going back," she'd said. She'd said nothing more after that, but he saw her drawn strained face when she came home from her evening vigil at his side, and the tension had not left her body. It was as he'd seen her only a few times in his life—whenever she had to follow a difficult course and knew she could. When she went back to work a few years ago, for example, and Jake was determined she wouldn't do it.

"I can support my family," he kept saying. "I don't want my wife working."

And after days of tension, her body stiff, her jaw set, she'd gone out and gotten a job. She didn't discuss things much, she just made up her mind and did them. Somehow he knew she'd made up her mind about Jake too. But he couldn't tell Bud that Jake might not come back.

"Griswold knows what he's doing," Jim said. "Remember when we had him as freshmen? You liked him then."

Bud threw the towel onto the pile in the corner and headed toward the locker room. "It was different then. We knew that in a year we'd get on the real team. We knew if we worked hard with Griswold, we'd make it. And we did."

Bud had worked that year, worked his tail off. But it didn't make him any better or any bigger. He was small and thin, too small for football, really. He almost didn't make the varsity.

Jim had gone to Jake. It was one of the hardest things he'd ever done, but for Bud he knew he could do it.

Jake was in the game room, surrounded by the trophies, staring at the television screen, though the set was not turned on. Jake often did that, sunk into a brood. He always claimed it was his thinking time, but somehow Jim knew he was brooding. Jim stood next to him, waiting to be noticed.

"What is it, boy? Spit it out."

"Dad, I want to ask you something. About the try-outs today."

Jake slid up in his chair, spread his knees, and put his large hands on them. "Yeah, yeah, I know what you're going to say. You were terrible today. It's like you never saw a football in your life. Hell, I was close to scrapping you after that first fumble. What's that lily-livered Griswold teaching you, anyway? You're worse than you were before you went in. I never should have left off coaching you myself. But don't worry. You're in."

"That—that wasn't it. I wasn't worrying about that."

"You weren't worrying about it? Well, boy, you should have worried about it. Just because you're my kid doesn't mean—"

"It's Bud Alden."

"Oh."

Jim looked at his father, at the lined face and the sunburned skin. He looked tired. "All his life Bud's waited for this moment, Dad."

"I know. If only he'd grown some. He's a shrimp. He should go out for track or gymnastics. He'd be good."

"But football's all he cares about. You know that."

Jake sighed. "I guess that's my fault. He seemed such a pathetic kid, no father and always hanging about, so I took him on when I took you on. I didn't know he'd turn out to be a shrimp."

"Every night, since we were eight or nine, remember?"

"I know. But I can't take him on the team. He's too small."

"He can run like hell. He's like a rabbit out there. You should see him in the freshman games. And he can tackle just by sheer surprise. But most of all, Dad, he needs it. You started coaching him so long ago, and it got in his blood. You got in his blood."

"He was rotten out there today. Everybody saw it. I can't take him on." Jake picked up the can of beer at his elbow and sipped it slowly, staring again at the blank TV screen.

It took all Jim's courage to say his next words, but they struck home. "If it was me, you'd do it."

Jake slammed down the can. A spray of foam bounced out the opening and splashed his face. "Don't you manipulate me, boy," he said. "I don't have the best goddamned team in the whole state for nothing, you know."

Jim dropped his gaze. He'd always found it difficult to look in his father's eyes. "I know, Dad—"

"I don't put guys on the team just because they happen to be buddies with my son. Understand?"

"But, Dad, that isn't the reason. Bud—"

"If you were five foot seven or whatever the hell he is, I wouldn't take you on either, son or no son." He turned his gaze away once more, looking this time at the portrait.

Jim stood there seething. It wasn't because Bud was his friend, that wasn't the reason. It was because of all those nights, the two boys and the man, practicing passes. Jake was as much a father to Bud as he was to Jim. If football was in Bud's blood, it was because of those nights, because of Jake.

"Besides," Jake said, "Bud's no good. God knows I've tried with him, but his mind wanders. He doesn't listen to the signals. He fumbles. What can I do with a clown like that on the team?"

"He tries, Dad. He works at it so hard."

His father nodded slowly. "Yeah. I guess that's true. Christ, if only he'd grown more. Why'd he turn out to be such a shrimp?"

The next day when the team list was posted, Bud's name was at the top.

"You know what really bugs me about Griswold?" Bud was saying. "He doesn't give a shit about football."

"Sure he does. He played in college. He coached somewhere else before he came here."

"Yeah, but he coaches swimming too. And he's into girls' gymnastics, would you believe? Took the team over to Porterville last month."

"They brought home a trophy, I hear."

Bud scoffed, then slipped on his shorts. "Do you know what Griswold told me once? He said I should go in for another sport. Said I was too small for football, the bastard."

Jim turned away so Bud wouldn't notice how he'd blushed. "What other sport did he suggest?"

"Track or swimming. Or gymnastics. It was just before tryouts when we were freshmen—after we'd been all season on the junior varsity. He took me aside and told me I had a lot of strengths—that I was quick, for one. But he said I wasn't big enough for football. Hell, I showed him, didn't I?"

Jim looked at his friend, the boy he'd known all his life. He remembered the nights in the vacant lot down the block with Jake coaching them, riding them both hard. Bud *was* too small for football, and it was beginning to tell. Jim wished he knew what to say, how to tell Bud he'd have to take a closer look at himself now that Coach wasn't around. With Griswold it wouldn't be so easy because Griswold didn't know him the way Jake did. Funny, Jim thought, as tough as his father was, he'd always had a soft spot for Bud.

Len Wilson came along, carrying his sport bag. "You guys in the mood for a hamburger at Mandy's?"

"Yeah, why not. It'll take the rotten taste out of my mouth," Bud said.

"Rotten taste? Man, that was our best practice yet."

"Yeah, no thanks to Bastard Griswold."

Len put his hand on Bud's arm. "Hey, fella, don't

blame the coach. You weren't with it out there, you know? He had to bench you. You've got to get your shit together, buddy."

Bud shook off Len's hand. "I don't need to get it together for him. Not for him." He went back toward the bathroom.

"What's with him?" Len said.

Jim sighed. "He had a special feeling for Dad. He's taking it awfully hard."

"I guess so. He's been playing worse than ever. Griswold had no choice but to bench him. Your dad always benched him too."

"I know. Bud Alden has more slivers in his butt than anybody on the team."

"Well, we'll try to cheer him up at Mandy's. You coming?"

"No thanks, Len. I'd better head on home."

"Whatever you say, man. By the way, some of us got to talking about Dundee at lunch. About you losing your cool and all."

"Oh, that." It seemed a year since his outburst.

"We're going over and see him tonight. At his apartment. Want to come?"

Jim didn't answer. He was remembering his dad in the men's room. He wondered how he could go back to the hospital, but he knew sometime he had to.

"Jim? You heard me, didn't you?"

"What?"

"We're going to fix Dundee. We're going to make it okay."

Jim shook his head absently. "Good, Len." Then, like a child at a party, suddenly remembering his manners, "Thanks, Len."

Len sat beside him. "Hey, what is it, man?"

Jim sorted through his mind for the appropriate response, some lie to tell Len, to get him off his back. Then he looked into the deep black eyes and saw the concern. "He's—he's suffering, Len. He's in awful pain, and I don't think he can take it."

"Your dad?"

"Yeah. I—I went there today. After Dundee's class, I couldn't take it anymore, and suddenly I wanted to see Dad. God, I don't know why. I'm so mixed up. I wish I hadn't."

"What happened?" Len asked softly.

"He wasn't in his room. So I went looking for him. The nurse took me to this solarium place. And he was in the men's room. He was crying, Len. My dad, cry-ing."

Len let out a low whistle. "Man, that's heavy. Coach Halbert letting someone see him cry."

"He didn't see me. He didn't know I was there."

"Then, how?"

"I went in, and I heard him in the john. But before he came out, I beat it."

"Then how'd you know it was him?"

"It was him. I'm positive."

"Why'd you leave?"

"I—I don't know. I guess I didn't want him to see me like that. I mean, I didn't want him to—Jesus, I don't know. I just ran."

"Maybe next time you should stay. Maybe he needs to have someone see him. He's been hiding it so long. It's a hell of a burden to carry alone, you know. Even for Coach."

"He wouldn't like it. Not like that. You know how he is, Len."

Len continued to stare at him, then he spoke, his voice little more than a whisper. "He needs you, Jim. No matter what he says, he needs you."

"He has a crazy way of showing it."

"Go over there again. Tonight. Now. Let him know you're there and that you know about the pain."

"I can't, Len. He—"

"Go, Jim. For your own sake as well as his."

Jim looked at his friend and finally nodded.

Len stood up just as Bud came back. "So, let's get on over to Mandy's," Bud said. "You coming, Jim?"

"No. I—I think I'll head over to the hospital and look in on Dad."

"Say hello to him, will you?" Bud said, his face suddenly serious.

"Come on, old buddy, let's not keep those greasy hamburgers waiting." Len clapped Jim on the shoulder, picked up his bag, and headed out, whistling.

15

Jim drove home first, thinking he might ask Liz if she wanted to go to the hospital with him. He wasn't certain he wanted to be alone with his father. Liz wasn't in her room, though her books were on her desk and her jacket was thrown across the bed.

He dropped his own books on his bed and stood for a moment looking at the telephone. He'd resolved to call Mimi, to clear the air and get back to normal. Later, he decided. After I've seen Dad and dealt with that.

Going with Gus to the Gulley didn't seem so ridiculous now. He smiled to himself, remembering how she'd laughed about the small back seat of his Volkswagen. "They're going to need a can opener to get us out of here," she'd said. For a moment, she'd made him forget, had taken away the pain. But he had to face it, face his dad, sort it out. He decided to grab a Coke from downstairs and head over to the hospital.

He took the basement steps two at a time and went straight to the refrigerator. He took out a Coke, opened it, and stood sipping it, gazing absently at the blank TV screen, thinking about Jake, about the past, Bud making the team, Jake hollering at him, the crisp evening air on the field, his father silhouetted against the sky, running, catching, laughing. Yes, his father had laughed too. He'd forgotten that. In the past two years since he'd joined the team, he'd seen so much of his father's anger, he'd forgotten the Jake who also laughed.

Suddenly he realized the TV screen wasn't blank at all. Reflected in the center of its curved gray surface was a face, its eyes studying him. "Liz?"

She didn't answer, but he heard her draw in her breath. He went around by the chair and there she was, sitting quietly in Jake's chair. She looked like a child, small in the corner of the chair, and she was hugging something like a doll. It was Jake's All-American trophy.

"What's the matter Lizzy?" Unconsciously he fell into the childhood name. "What's happened?"

"Nothing. Nothing at all. I came down to get a Coke. And then I saw that old bicycle sitting there. And then the trophies, and suddenly—" Her voice wavered and she started to cry. She put her face against the cold metal of the trophy and cried.

Jim stood motionless, unable to comfort her.

When she'd finished, she sniffed, wiped the trophy with her sleeve, and stood up. "Look at the dust on this thing. Nobody ever dusts down here. It's like a pigpen." She put the trophy in its place, then ran her finger along the edge of the shelf, coming up with a small pile of dust.

"Dad won't let Mom do it. Afraid she'll break his precious—I mean, his trophies. And of course he wouldn't do it himself," Jim said.

" 'The little toy dog is covered with dust—' "

"What?"

She shrugged. "A silly poem I learned as a kid. About a boy who dies, and they leave the room with all his toys, all dusty and rotting away. That's what this is like. I wonder if we'll just leave it this way. Afterward. Like a memorial or something."

"Liz, don't."

"I suppose we will. Maybe people will come from all over the state—maybe even the whole country—to gaze on the trophies and look at the portrait." She studied it, then looked at Jim. "Must have driven him crazy."

"What?"

"You look so much like him. I guess that was most of it."

"Most of what?"

"Why he went at you the way he did. Every night as long as I can remember, you and Bud in the vacant lot, and later over to the field. He sure wanted to make a player out of you."

"Yes."

"But it didn't work."

"Hey, Liz, I'm not as bad as all that. Come on."

She smiled. "No, that isn't what I meant. He wanted so much for you to be like him. To care about football the way he does. Mom used to say he ate, drank, and slept football. Still does. And these trophies down here—they mean more to him than anything else. More than us, I think, sometimes. I bet if he could, he'd have us stuffed and put down here. You, at least." She looked again at the portrait. "You sure do look like him. But there's something missing." She glanced at Jim. "It's the eyes. Remember in that old movie about the Ten Commandments and Charlton Heston comes down from the mountain? And they say something like, 'Look at his eyes—he's seen God.' There's something like that in Dad's eyes, you know? Like he's seen something nobody else has, something nobody else understands."

Jim had seen that shadow in the eyes of his father's portrait, but he'd thought it was fear. It wasn't. It was surprise—awe. Like Liz said, he'd seen God.

"Oh, brother! What got me going?" Liz said.

"I'm going over to the hospital. Want to come?"

She waited a long time before answering. "No."

"Why not? You've hardly been there."

"I know. It's just that, well, it's too hard. Seeing him like that. I know, I'm being selfish again. I've been a bitch through this whole thing, but I can't stand to see him flat on his back with those bottles hanging over him. I don't know what I'm going to do when it gets worse. And it will." She started to cry again.

"What's hardest," she sobbed, "is the way he acts. I mean, here I am crying like a fool, and he's the one who ought to be crying. He's the one it's happening to. But he goes on as if nothing's happened. Even in the hospital, putting on a show."

Jim remembered his father sobbing in the hospital bathroom—alone where no one could see him. But he didn't tell Liz about that, about their father's lonely struggle with his pain.

She raised her head and pulled away from Jim's embrace. She looked at the trophies again. "You know, in a way I hate these things. I'd like to take the lot of them and smash them against the wall."

"Why, Liz?"

"Because they'll be here after he's gone." She turned and left the room.

Jim stood sipping the last of his Coke and thinking. Liz was right. The trophies would be here—or somewhere else—for a long, long time. The golden figures, nearly a complete team by now, would never throw those forward passes. The passes would never miss or be intercepted. His father would die, and Jim in turn would die, too. But the trophies would go on. Was that all that lasted? A pile of tawdry metal? Is that what it came down to in the end?

Just then the phone rang. He waited a moment for Liz to answer, but she didn't, so he picked up the downstairs extension.

"Hello, stranger. It's Mimi."

Her voice should have cheered him, but somehow it depressed him all the more. "Hello, Mimi."

"I decided to swallow my pride and call you. I got to thinking maybe you didn't get my message the other night."

"I—I got it. I was too upset about Dad. And then, you'd said not to call again, so—"

"I was mad at you. I didn't really mean it. I just wanted you to know how pissed I was."

"Yes, well, I got your message."

"I saw the guys at Mandy's tonight. They're all hyped up about the game tomorrow. So we got to knocking around a few ideas, and I came home and wrote a special cheer. For tomorrow. I wanted to tell you about it."

"All right."

"I mean, not now. I want it to be a surprise."

"Oh. Look, Mimi, I'm going over to the hospital right now. Maybe we could talk later."

"How is your dad? The guys were talking about him, but they don't know how he's doing. Bud

Alden's really shook up about the whole thing. I don't blame him, I guess. Everybody's pretty down this year, you know?"

"Dad's doing all right, I guess. I haven't seen him for a couple of days, but Mom goes over there every night after work. Look, Mimi, I do want to see you again. I mean, I've been meaning to call in spite of what you said, but I don't know, I've just been bumbling around like a fool. This whole thing's got me spinning my wheels, getting nowhere, you know what I mean?"

"Sure, Jim, I understand. I mean, if I can't understand about that, then what good am I? But don't forget me, Jimbo. If you need a shoulder to cry on, I've got a broad one. Well, not really, but you know what I mean."

Jim laughed, thinking about Mimi's rounded breast. Yes, he knew what she meant, and yes, he did want to lay his head there. Very much. "Look, after the scrimmage tomorrow, why don't we go out? Take in a movie or something. Try to get it all back together."

"Oh, Jim, I was hoping you'd say that. I've missed you so. Everybody's always asking me about you—I mean, you're just about the most famous guy at school these days—and I have to hem and haw around. I think people are starting to think we've broken up. Let's stop by Mandy's first. Everybody'll be going there. Then they can see for themselves that nothing's changed."

Mimi and her fear of change, Jim thought. Every-thing is falling apart about our ears, and Mimi's con-vincing herself nothing's changed. "Okay. I'll meet you on the field after the game."

Jim went upstairs. Liz's music was pulsating from her room. He knew it was no good asking her again.

Once in the car, he drove aimlessly, heading first toward Mandy's, then turning around halfway and heading back home, then driving right past the house. He didn't want to go to the hospital and yet he knew he should.

His mind was swirling. He ran a stop sign near the school and came close to ramming a car. They ex-changed horn blasts and the car sped on, leaving Jim alone and shaken. He shouldn't be driving. It was a good thing he didn't go on the highway.

He looked over at the school. The parking lot was, of course, empty, the spotlights on the corners of the building the only light. He got out and walked onto the school grounds, heading around the building to-ward the football field.

The white lines of the grid were all that gave the field substance. He felt almost that if he stepped out, he'd fall through, not find solid ground. He looked at the goalpost at the far end, remembering the day he'd run in that score.

It had been good, that part of it—feeling the rhythm of his cleats striking the turf, churning it up, and the deep, even breathing. Feeling the ball cradled like a child in his arms, knowing it was his and he was taking it all the way home. Then the guys hoisting him on their shoulders and carrying him back across the field, the crowd's cheers in his ears. It was afterward, when Jake's face had loomed like a great balloon in front of him and the words "Saturday hero" had drowned out the cheers—that's when it all turned sour.

Suddenly he wanted to run.

He stepped out onto the field, the turf slightly damp with evening dew. He walked swiftly, then broke into a jogtrot, and finally a run. Unconsciously he curled his right arm as if the football were there again. He could almost feel its nubbed surface under his fingertips. The whistle of the wind in his ears was like the cheering of a large crowd. Then as his pace became regular, the imagined cheering became a chant. *"Hal-bert, Hal-bert, Hal-bert!"* Halbert was the star of the team, they knew him, they remembered his 95-yard touchdown last year. And he was back. He'd have a glorious season and then he'd go on—to Penn State, maybe on a scholarship, it was possible. And then, pro ball? The Dolphins?

As his mind played out the fantasy, another level seemed to run concurrently, deeper, like the bass line of a concerto. Someone else had run on this field, carried the ball to the cheers of the crowd. And the crowd had called *"Halbert"* then too. They'd called for Jake—James Kenneth Halbert—and the fantasy had been real.

Jim tripped on a hillock and went spinning. He lay on the frosted ground, the air knocked out of him and his knee twinging where he'd tried to break his fall.

When he'd caught his breath, he rolled over on his back and looked up at the sky. The clouds hung low, threatening rain. Probably by tomorrow's game the field would be awash with mud. But tomorrow's game was a long time away.

He smiled to himself; grinned, in fact. He felt peaceful and joyful, excited and calm. What he'd felt the day he ran in the touchdown was love. He'd felt a group of people rise up and give him love. And whatever happened after that didn't really matter, not when he'd known that love. He'd felt it again tonight in his imagination—a ghost of that love haunting the field. Well, why not? This patch of churned-up turf had seen a lot of action in the sixty-odd years the school had been here. Some great players had run here—his father the greatest of them. Why couldn't the ghosts of the crowd haunt the stands at night when no one was around? The love was great enough, why not?

He sat up, shaking his head. Here he was lying on

the damp ground in the middle of the night thinking about ghosts. What kind of a nurd was he, anyway?

He got up and headed, at a walk this time, back across the field. How crazy was it, after all? Even if the ghosts weren't real, the love was. And that's what it was all about—football. That's why guys got themselves bashed about like bull elephants—to feel the joy of the crowd's cheering. To feel the love. And once you've felt it—the way Jim did once, and the way his father must have over and over—well, there was no letting go. You had to chase after that love in game after game. That was the reason his father "ate, drank, and slept football," as his mother said.

For some reason, one of Dundee's poems came into his mind.

> So set, before its echoes fade,
> The fleet foot on the sill of shade,
> And hold to the low lintel up
> The still defended challenge-cup.

Yes, the trophies would outlast Jake; they'd outlast Jim too. But they weren't the only lasting things. The love would last. The love of the crowd, and a more important love. His own love for his father, now that he understood what made him tick.

16

Jim stood outside Room 23 for a moment, almost afraid to go in. The glow of his run was still on him. Finally he pushed the door open.

His mother was in a chair pulled up to his father's bedside, but the bed was empty. Her head was bowed, her hands lying limp in her lap.

"Mom? Where's Dad?"

She looked up, startled. "Jim? I wasn't expecting you." One hand pushed back a strand of hair, the other smoothed her skirt.

"Where's Dad?" he asked again, his hands out as if to grab her shoulders and shake her. "Has something happened?" *Is it too late?* his mind screamed. *Did I wait too long to learn I loved him?*

"Happened? No, Jim, nothing. He's gone for some tests. He was feeling weak tonight and couldn't eat his dinner."

Jim sighed and sank onto the bed. "God, I thought—"

"Thought what?"

He shook his head. "Nothing. Just seeing you here—the empty bed—" He let his voice trail off.

She cupped his hand with her own. "He's all right, Jim. Don't worry."

"I—there's so much, Mom, I want to tell him. I drove like a madman to get here. I—I was afraid when I saw you—" He felt the tears coming. He let them flow.

She drew him toward her and held his head against her breast, letting him cry the way he did when he was little. She made soothing sounds in his ear and rocked his head gently.

Finally, he looked up. "There's so much I have to tell him," he said again.

"Later, Jim. Not tonight. He'll be too tired when he gets back."

Just then the swinging door opened, and two nurses came in wheeling a stretcher. Jake lay flat on it, his eyes closed, an intravenous bottle swinging over his head. Jim and his mother moved out of the way. With quick, efficient movements, the nurses lifted Jake onto the bed, attached the I.V., and slid the stretcher away. One nurse left with it, glancing briefly at Jim. The other stayed at Jake's side, taking his pulse. Jake did not stir or open his eyes.

"How is he?" Jim's mother asked the nurse.

She finished taking his pulse, then patted him on the shoulder and straightened the blankets. "He's fine," she said, "but heavily sedated. He'll sleep the night."

Jim stepped forward. "But I've got to talk to him. I've got to tell him—"

His mother put her arm around his waist. "Not tonight, Jim. Let's go home and see about some dinner." She led him away from the bed and out into the hall.

"Is your sister at home?" she asked.

"Liz? Yes. She was earlier, anyway." He remembered Liz's words in the game room. He was sorry he'd left without a word.

"I'm surprised you didn't bring her with you," his mother was saying. "Though I guess it's just as well."

"Liz didn't want to come. She was pretty upset tonight."

They had reached the parking lot and stood under one of the glaring lights. "Upset?"

"Yes. She was down in the trophy room. It's hard on her, Mom. She loved him so much. Loves him, I mean."

"Then I'd think she'd want to be with him as much as possible."

"It hurts her that he won't open up more. That he keeps on pretending the way he does."

His mother sighed. "It's a hard lesson to learn, Jim. Your dad can't let down his defenses. Never could. Can't admit to a weakness. I've lived with him for nearly twenty years, and I don't think I've ever heard him cry."

Jim tried to find the words to tell her about what had happened earlier that day in the bathroom, and later at the field. He wanted her to know. But somehow he couldn't work out how to say it.

"You look more like him every day," she was saying. "You look just like he did the day I met him. It frightens me."

"Frightens you?"

"Yes. I don't want you to be like him, Jim. I love him, but I don't want you to be like him. He holds back too much. He won't give enough of himself. Except, of course, to the game. There's always enough for football."

"I know, Mom, but there's a reason. Tonight on the field, I—"

She went on as if he hadn't spoken. "And now, when there's so little time left, all he can talk about is going back there, back on that field. I can't stand it, Jim. I don't think I can take it anymore."

It was Jim's turn to comfort her. "He has to, Mom. I understand about that now. I wish I could tell you what happened tonight."

"I want some time with him. I want to be with him as long as I can. I don't want to share him with that team anymore, with that school. Maybe we could go somewhere. We've never traveled much."

"Why don't you ask him about it? Maybe he'd like it."

"No. He'll only tell me he can't leave now. Not

during the season. And it's always the season. I've lived long enough with him to know that."

She turned and headed toward her car. Jim watched her, wishing, as he had earlier with Liz, that he had the right words to say. But he realized there was no way he could ease her grief, or Liz's. Only his own, maybe.

17

Jim got off with a reprimand for cutting school all afternoon. He told the principal when he was called down that he'd felt claustrophobic and just had to get away. He didn't mention his father but sat tight-lipped in the office, giving no more details. Mr. Weaver's eyes stayed on Jim's face a little too long, and he nodded. He suggested next time Jim get a pass, but he wrote nothing on the report in front of him. Jim left feeling slightly soiled.

As he rounded the corner he saw Gus foraging in the tangle of books and papers at the bottom of her locker. "Hi," he said.

She glanced up. He realized her dark eyes were shining with tears. She blinked them away, and the cynical grin took over her mouth. "Hey, fellow convict. Are you kicked out, too?"

"Kicked out?"

"Yeah. Suspended is the word they use—as in

hanging. 'Course in my case it might as well be expelled. I'm not coming back."

"Suspended? Gus! You were suspended? For yesterday?"

She pulled out her math book, took her jacket off the hook, and slammed the locker shut. Papers, like lettuce from a sandwich, seeped out the edges. "I'm taking this book back to Mr. Bowden. The rest can just come and get them for themselves." She turned. "How long you suspended for?" she asked him.

"I—I'm not."

She raised an eyebrow and cocked her head to one side. "You're not? But they gave me three days. And we were together."

"I know. It doesn't make sense."

"Yes, it does. In Woods Cross, it makes sense." She pushed past him and started down the hall. "See you around."

"Gus, wait."

She turned again. In the dim light of the hallway, her face looked translucent, as if she would disappear any moment. "What?"

"If you're suspended, I'm suspended."

"You said you weren't."

He raised one hand. "I hereby suspend myself."

She smiled. "You can't do that. It has to be done officially. After all, this is Woods Cross. Things are done by the book here."

"So, do it by the book."

She tossed her hair back and scowled, scanning her math book as if it were a report. "Let me see, let me see. You must be John—"

"Jim. Jim Halbert."

"Oh, yes, that's right. Now, what can I do for you?" She adjusted imaginary glasses on her nose and peered through them.

Jim cleared his throat. "You sent for me, sir."

"Oh, that's right, that's right. What for, I wonder?" She scanned her math book again. "It must be here somewhere. Everything is in these reports."

"Could it be because of yesterday?"

"Yesterday? Yes, it must have been. What happened yesterday?"

By this time Jim was laughing out loud. "Get on with it. I haven't got all day."

"Yes, certainly. Kneel down."

"Kneel down?"

When he was kneeling, Gus lifted her math book and whopped him on the shoulder. "You are hereby officially suspended," she announced, knocking him to the floor. Jim laughed.

"You're crazy, Agnes Palmer."

Gus sat beside him. "He kept calling me *Agatha*. He couldn't even get my name right."

Just then Mr. Dundee turned the corner suddenly and nearly stepped on them. "What the—Jim? What is this? Some kind of sit-down strike?"

Jim scrambled to his feet and helped Gus up. "No, sir. We were just—"

"Because if it is, I'd like to join you. I've had it up to here." Dundee laughed good-naturedly, but Jim noticed an edge to his laughter. "In fact, you're just the person I've been wanting to see."

"I—uh—I've been suspended, sir. I'm supposed to leave the building right away."

Gus looked at him quizzically, but he put his hand on her arm to keep her from saying anything.

"Suspended? You?"

He nodded. "So, I'd better get going."

"Come here. I want to talk with you. Let's find a corner of the library."

"But—"

"Look, Jim," Gus said. "I've got to find Mr. Bowden and give him this book. I'll meet you somewhere."

"My car."

He followed Dundee into the library. They found a table and Jim settled across from him.

"I had a visit last night. A contingency of students from AP English. Led by Len Wilson."

Jim met Dundee's blue eyes squarely, but said nothing.

"Do you know what they wanted?"

Jim remembered what Len had told him in the locker room, but he decided not to share it with Dundee, not to share anything with Dundee if he could help it. "Not really, sir."

"They said I was to blame for what happened yesterday. For your—uh—outburst in class. They said I had it coming." He leaned back and took a deep breath. His hand where it lay on the table was trembling. "What's this about you being suspended? That have anything to do with me?"

"I skipped school yesterday. After your class, as a matter of fact."

"So it did have to do with me."

"Not really, sir."

"They shouldn't suspend you. I can talk to Mr. Weaver."

"I don't want you to do that, sir."

"Will you stop 'sirring' me? You sound like a preppy." The outburst caused a stir in the library. Quickly Dundee lowered his voice and leaned forward, spreading his hands flat on the table. "Level with me, Jim. Have I been hassling you? Like the kids said?"

Jim thought back to the day before, amazed that it had only been one day since he had stormed out of English class. Since then he'd seen his father cry and heard the cheers of his father's crowd. Since then he'd learned his mother's burden. What did it matter anymore about Dundee and his unit on death?

"Tell me something," Jim said. "Did your father really hang himself from a Ferris wheel?"

Dundee raised his chin as if to ward off a blow. "What's that got to do with—"

"Nothing, really. I'd just like to know."

Dundee lowered his head. "Yes."

"How old were you?"

"Nine. No, ten."

"And that part about the fish. Was that true?"

He studied Jim's face for a long time. "What has this to do with what we were talking about, Jim?"

"I guess it has to do with honesty, sir. I mean, Mr. Dundee."

Dundee stared at him, then batted his pale lashes and said in a whisper. "No. I didn't break the fish tank."

"Was there a fish tank?"

"Yes. That part was true. I know how it must have looked—the dead fish in the tank yesterday. But I honestly didn't see the fish until that moment. In fact, I don't think I ever drew the connection at all between that fish tank and the one in the principal's office." He covered his face with his hands. When he drew them away, his eyes were flooded with tears. "I wanted to break that tank. I wanted to do something beside sit there alone like a jerk. And after a while I began to believe I had done it, had broken the tank and made everybody come running. Even in my dreams I've seen that glass breaking, that water gushing out onto the floor, the fish with their mouths gaping. But after you shouted at me yesterday I went home and thought about it. What I really did was puke. Right there in the principal's office. All over his desk." He paused and they sat in silence.

Finally Dundee spoke again. "I was angry, Jim. Angry enough to break a hundred fish tanks. But not at the principal. I was angry at my father. For doing what he did. A Ferris wheel, for God's sake! A wire service picked it up. It was in all the papers across the country. Nearly killed my mother. And when I had to go back to school, it was hell. The other kids wouldn't say anything, but they knew all about it. It was their not saying that drove me up the wall."

Jim looked up, recognizing the feeling. "I know. That's what it's like for me."

"Yes. I know. But with your dad, Jim, it's different. You have nothing to be ashamed of."

At first Jim was angry. He wanted to shout at Dundee again for saying such a thing, for even suggesting that he would be ashamed. But then he realized Dundee was not talking about him, but about himself and his own shame. Even now, years later, his cheeks burned with the shame.

"I *was* ashamed at first," he told Dundee. "I wished he wouldn't come to school and let everybody see him. But I'm not anymore. I hope he'll be back. I hope he'll go on as long as he can." As he heard his words, Jim realized how true they were. One part of him felt the betrayal of his mother's dreams, but an-

other, more honest part of him knew the truth of what
he said.

"You haven't answered my question yet, Jim.
Have I been hassling you?"

"Yes. But it's okay. I can deal with it now."

"I have a decision to make, then. I've never been
too comfortable with this unit. There *was* a sea gull in
Bermuda, Jim, just as there *was* a fish tank. I'd been
wanting to do a unit on death for several years, but the
head of the department wasn't too keen on it. Then,
when I saw the sea gull and realized how I felt about
it, I decided to go ahead. I worked hard putting the
thing together. When I got to school and found out
about your father, I was torn in two trying to decide
whether to go ahead with it. Especially when I realized you were in the class. But I decided to be honest.
That was, after all, the whole point of doing the unit.
You were wrong when you said I planned it because
of your father's illness, Jim. I wouldn't have done that.
And I probably shouldn't have started it when I found
out about him."

Jim didn't answer, but he did believe him.

"I realized something else too," Dundee went on.
"About honesty. I realized I hadn't really faced my
own feelings about death—about my father's death.
My anger. It wasn't until I stood up there yesterday
telling you about breaking that fish tank that I realized
how angry I'd been. How angry I still am. The other

poem we read—the Dylan Thomas one. Do you remember it?"

"No." Jim's mind had been wandering at that
point in class. He hadn't tuned in again until Dundee
began the story of his father.

" 'Do not go gentle into that good night.' " Dundee
quoted, " 'rage, rage against the dying of the light.'
Death is full of rage, Jim. Anger is an important part
of grief."

Jim thought about his own anger and then about
Liz's. Liz said she wanted to smash all the trophies.
Dundee wanted to smash the fish tank. What had
he wanted to smash? Then he remembered the fury
the night he threw the ball at his father, and he
knew.

"At least I got the anger out of you," Dundee said.
"I thought yesterday you were going to smash my face
in. And I wouldn't have blamed you."

Jim smiled for the first time.

The bell rang and the students in the library
headed toward the door. Dundee stood up. "Well,
there they go. Pavlov's dogs salivating to the bell.
Don't you have a class?"

"I—uh—"

"Oh, that's right. You're suspended. Look, let me
clear that up with Mr. Weaver."

"No, sir. I mean, Mr. Dundee. The truth is, I'm
not exactly suspended."

"Not exactly suspended? Is that like being a little bit pregnant?"

"I mean, I'm not officially suspended. I suspended myself. As a sort of protest."

Mr. Dundee studied him for a moment, then smiled. "Well, have it your own way, Jim. But if you need a pass, you know where to find me." He joined the crowd leaving the library.

18

Gus was sitting on the curb next to Jim's car leafing through her math book. "You took your sweet time," she said good-naturedly.

"He had a lot to say. But I'm finished now." He indicated her math book. "Couldn't you find Bowden?"

"Yeah, I found him. But he wouldn't take the book. Said I'd be back. I told him I wouldn't. All I have to do is tell my dad I'm suspended, and I'm out of school. Mr. Bowden's a nice guy. Ever since that first day when you helped me with the assignment and I did good, he's been really super to me. But he doesn't know my dad."

They got in the car and Jim started the engine. "Hungry?"

"Yeah. I could use a cup of coffee, anyhow." She dug a cigarette out of her bag and lit it. Jim headed for Mandy's.

Across the table in the quiet lunchroom, Gus studied Jim. "You know, you shouldn't be doing this,
going with me. I mean, you'll be suspended for sure
this time. Maybe even worse."

"I should have been anyway. If they suspended
you, they should have suspended me."

"I think it was because of all the other times with
me. You know, getting kicked out of class, smoking
in the girls' room, and of course, that fight in
the lunchroom. Cutting yesterday was the final
straw."

"They should have called us down together—gotten the whole story. I mean, you did it for me. You
went with me because you knew I needed someone
with me. They should have asked you where you
went."

Gus laughed. "Now, you don't want to give them
the *whole* story, do you?"

Jim blushed. "I'm sorry. I'd forgotten about the
Gulley. I mean—"

"You mean, you'd forgotten about the Gulley."
She shrugged her thin shoulders and stubbed out her
cigarette.

Jim took her hand. "I hadn't forgotten, Gus. Stop
putting yourself down. I just meant I'd forgotten that
was part of our cutting yesterday." He kneaded the
long fingers.

She smiled. "Jim, I want you to know something. I

want to say it straight, no apologies, no bullshit, okay?"

"Okay."

"Yesterday was one super thing. I mean it. I'd never had anything like that, not like that. I've had it, sure—in the back of pickups in West Virginia a few times. But I'd never had it like with you. Gentle and special. But I know it wasn't because of me. It was because of what you're going through—with your father and all. And it doesn't matter. And you don't owe me anything." She drained her coffee cup and slid out of the booth. "I'm going to fetch another cup and one of those sticky buns Mandy has up there. Want anything?"

"I'll get it." He started to get up.

"No. I want to talk to Mandy, anyway." She stood for a long time, leaning against the counter smoking and chatting with the old man. When she came back, she had two cups of coffee and two sticky buns on top of the cups, balancing them expertly like a trained waitress. "I got me a job," she announced. "Starting today."

"A job?"

"Yeah. Mandy needs someone to wait tables in this joint. It'd make a big difference, you know. This business of going after your own, hell, it's like McDonalds only not as good. I talked him into taking me on to wait the tables for lunch and then later when the kids come in. For tips only, of course, but it's a start."

"But, Gus, you're still in school. I can see it for the afternoon, but lunch?"

"I'll have to get a work permit, of course. But I'm over sixteen so there ain't no law that says I can't quit school."

"Gus, you can't quit. You're only a year away from graduation."

She smiled, rather like an indulgent teacher with a backward child. "I'm never going to graduate, Jim. It isn't just my dad. I mean, he'll raise hell when he finds out I got suspended, but, of course, there's no reason he's got to find out. But it's me. I'm flunking every class except math. Crazy when you think about it. It's math I ought to be flunking, but you helped me get started with that, and of course, there's Bowden. I'll miss him, you know? But I might as well quit and get it over with."

"Gus, you're out of your mind. You've been in school exactly two weeks and already you're quitting?"

"It's more than flunking classes and getting suspended. I just don't fit in at Woods Cross and I never will."

"Give it time, Gus. You're in too big a hurry for everything."

She cocked her head to one side. "Yeah, that's been said before. But, Jim, I'm country, and no matter

where I go, I'll still be country. Those kids know that.
You know it. I mean, you're a hell of a nice guy, but I
know what I am. Even Len Wilson knows what I am."

"Len Wilson? How did he get into this?"

"When he took me home from the hospital the
other night, he got to talking about what it was like for
him when he first came, you know, the only black in
the whole school. But there's a difference between him
and me. He's got class. Take the way he dresses, for
example, and the way he talks. Even where I come
from, they'd be able to see that."

"You've got class too, Gus. More class than most of
those kids."

"Hell, Jim, you don't have to bullshit me. I know
what I am."

"I'm not bullshitting you, Gus. You're honest.
You're straight. And that's better than most people.
Better than me."

She lowered her head, letting her thin hair fall over
her face. In anyone else, it might have been to hide a
blush, but Jim didn't think Gus would blush.

When she looked up, her face was as pale as ever.
"But there's another matter to settle."

"What's that?"

"You. I want you to get back to school. As soon as
we finish here."

"I'm suspended for three days, remember?"

"You're not. And don't say you should be, because

you shouldn't be. I thought about it while I was waiting for you. They didn't suspend you for a lot of reasons. One of them was because of your dad."

"I know. The old sympathy bit. I could do most anything short of burning the school down, and I'd get off. That bugs me, you know?"

"I know. But it's the way it is. So why not ride with it?"

"Because it isn't fair. If your dad were dying, you'd understand."

"I do understand. But what's the point of cutting again? What'll it prove?"

"That they can't treat me that way. That justice should be meted out fairly." He heard his own voice and frowned. He sounded like Dundee.

"Where is it written it's gotta be fair?"

Jim took a deep breath. "I know. I've heard that before. But that doesn't mean we have to live with it. Have to go on taking it."

"Okay. Suit yourself. If you want to cut school, cut school. But it's for yourself, not for me. Remember that."

"I will."

"Good. You might as well get going then, wherever you're going. I've got to go home and clean up. I've got work to do."

"But I thought we'd spend the day together."

"Nope. Have to work. Anyway, don't you have a game today?"

"Yes, the first of the season, why?" A game, and then a date with Mimi. Jesus.

"Course, you can't play."

"Can't play? Why not?"

"You're suspended."

"Jesus."

She laughed. "Forgot about that, didn't you?"

"Yes. I—I've got to play. I mean, it's our first game, and Dad'll be counting on—I mean, I've got to play."

"So, go back to school." She grinned.

Jim took a deep breath. "Okay, I'll make a deal with you. If I go back today, will you come back after three days? Give it another try?"

"I told you. I don't fit in at Woods Cross."

"Bullshit. You don't want to fit in, that's all. Len makes it not just because he's smart but because he buys the system. Maybe that's not honest, and I just got through telling you that what I like best about you is your honesty. But instead of bucking the system all the time, why not give it a chance? You go into the girls' room and smoke, knowing full well you'll get caught. You talk out in study so you'll get thrown out. You revel in being different. And that's being just as phony as the other kids are." He caught his breath.

She stared at him, her eyes large with surprise, then she lowered her head once more. "Shit," she said quietly, almost to herself.

"Gus—"

"Get out of here."

"But, Gus—"

"Go on, get out. You creep. You're just as bad as the rest. What do you know about anything, anyway?"

"I'm sorry, Gus. I lost my temper. I—"

She looked up. Her eyes were bright with tears and a red patch spread across her cheek like a birthmark. "I said get out. Get lost. Get off my case."

"I—I'll go back to school, Gus. Like you said."

"I don't give a shit where you go. You can go to hell." She slid out of the booth and went toward the back, toward the ladies' room, taking her beaded bag with her.

He waited for a moment, staring at the cold coffee turning greasy in the bottom of the cup. Finally he slid out and left Mandy's. He headed back to school.

19

Jim was lacing up his cleats when Len came up. "How're you feeling?"

"Okay. You been out there?"

Len always took a look at the opposition just before a game. He could be counted on for a report of the size of the boys, and more important, some quality that only Len seemed able to spot—team spirit.

"Yeah. They're big. Look like real contenders this year. But we have a chance. If we get it together."

"Think we can?"

Len looked serious. He joined Jim on the bench. "Griswold's done a good job, whipped us into a team when before we were just a rabble. Except for Alden. He's still bucking. We can try, at least, but we're missing something. Alden's right about that, though it's not Griswold's fault the way he says."

"What? Team spirit, I suppose."

"That's a bullshit word. We lack drive. Coach al-

ways gave us that. It'd take more than a week for anyone else to give us that. Maybe it's anger. Maybe we're
just not angry enough. I don't know. By the way,
Dundee dropped that death thing. He made a speech
in class today. Said he realized he'd been hassling you.
And that he wasn't being honest. That maybe you
really can't be honest about a thing like death. I mean,
man, it was a heavy scene."

"I can imagine," Jim said, not unkindly. "He told
me about you guys going to see him last night."

"Yeah, well, we felt we ought to level with him,
you know. He's not a bad guy, really. I think he was
just on the wrong track."

"I appreciate it, Len. I really do."

Len put his hand on Jim's shoulder. "You see your
dad?"

"Yes, but he was asleep. I'll go tonight after the
game."

"Then we'd better give those guys hell. Suit up
and I'll walk out with you. Griswold's about to deliver
his pep talk."

The pep talk was not like Jake's, but then no one
expected Griswold to call them names and swear at
them the way Jake did. Griswold's voice, as always,
was soft, his manner restrained. Slouched over, a little
shy, he seemed more like a college professor than a
football coach.

"I know you guys are uptight," he said. "Your first

game. You did well in practice, though. Don't forget that. And don't forget something else. You know how to play. Some of you have been playing for Woods Cross for three years—starting with me as freshmen. And you've had two years of Jake Halbert. That ought to make a football player out of a mouse."

They chuckled. Jim noticed that Bud Alden didn't laugh, but stared stonily at Griswold.

"What Jake left you is a legacy, and I want to see you carry it out there today."

It was an unfortunate choice of words. Suddenly, like air from a punctured tire, the spirit went out of the team.

Bud said it for all of them. "He ain't dead yet."

"I—I didn't mean that, fellas. I meant, playing today I want you to keep in mind the spirit that Jake built into you—built into the team."

"He'll be back," Bud continued. "He'll be back, don't worry. You don't need to start moving your things into his office. And don't go talking about him as if he was dead."

Bud's words did what Griswold's didn't. The boys began to shout, to wave their fists.

"For Coach!" chimed in another boy, and soon they were all shouting, "For Coach! Win this one for Coach!" In this spirit they soared out onto the field. The roar went up from the crowd on the bleachers.

Jim was proud of Bud, but wished he would accept

Griswold. Eventually he'd have to. In some ways Griswold was a better coach. He knew strategy and he knew psychology. But Griswold didn't know how to insult the boys, didn't know how to make them angry. And anger was what got the adrenalin going and turned them into bulls. They needed that to take the games the way they had all those years. Griswold treated them with respect. Maybe that would work after a while when they got used to it, but not now, in Jake's shadow. So Bud had given them anger.

They threw a few practice passes, then settled on the bench. The bleachers were full. Jim noticed there was a microphone set up near where Mimi and her cheerleaders were scampering. He wondered about it, then let his thoughts wander. It seemed strange to have the bleachers full. The last time he'd looked at those bleachers, Gus had been perched up there, her thin limbs drawn together, looking like a scrawny bird perched on a wire. Gus. Suddenly he missed her, longed for her with an intensity that was almost painful. She'd been so angry when he left her at Mandy's. Somehow he'd broken through her hard shell and touched a vulnerable part. He'd hurt her.

Someone turned the microphone on, and Mimi's cheers were suddenly amplified. Jim looked across at her. The white sweater with the large blue *W.C.* emphasized her rounded breasts, the *W* curving across one, the *C* across the other. His eyes lingered on those letters and his hands twitched, wanting to touch her. Thoughts of pathetic old Gus fled from his mind.

Mimi's blue and white skirt was short, coming to the top of her thighs. When she jumped up, holding the pom-poms over her head, the skirt flew up and her blue leotards tightened over her rounded hips. She saw him looking at her and waved. Then she walked up to the mike. Her voice, breathless and high-pitched, rang out across the field. The crowd quieted down.

"We have a special cheer we'd like to do," she said. There was a rustle of questioning behind Jim, and on the other side he could see the visitors shifting impatiently. Their own cheerleaders in brown and yellow stood with their hands on their hips. They watched, but they looked as if they might interrupt Mimi's special cheer with one of their own.

"As you know," Mimi went on, her voice wavering with nervousness, "our coach, Jake Halbert, is very, very sick. We wish he could be with us today because this is the first game. But we know he's with us in spirit. And because of that, because of Coach, I've—I mean, we've—made up a special cheer. We'd like the Elmwood visitors to join in with us. It goes like this."

She looked back at the other three girls on her squad. They nodded and held their pom-poms out, waiting.

"Coach Jake, you've got what it takes. . ." As Mimi spoke, her words clear, the girls with the pom-poms raised their arms, then brought them down slowly.

"The team'll give all they've got to give. And we won't forget you as long as you live. Geez, I got that wrong." The mike squealed as she blew into it. "Let's take it again, and I'll get it right, okay?" She giggled, cleared her throat, and started over.

"The team'll give all they've got to give. And we won't forget you as long as we live."

The mike screeched again with feedback as she shouted directly into it, "To Coach! To Coach! To Coach!"

The girls finished their gyrations and the crowd, stunned at first, began to cheer.

Jim stared at Mimi in disbelief. It was one thing to form her "conspiracy of honor"—it hadn't succeeded too well anyway and was mostly ignored. But to stand up there in front of the whole school—in front of another school as well—and practically bury him. And what she'd done with it—the way she'd mangled it. He wondered if, for people like Mimi, there wasn't a truth in the misstatement "we won't forget you as long as *you* live." It was like Griswold's choice of the word "legacy." Maybe Bud was right to be angry. It was as if the vultures were gathering, waiting for the right moment before swooping down.

A roar went up from the opposite bleachers as

their team scrambled onto the field. Jim was picked up in the rush of his own team and found himself on the field, waiting for the kickoff. Len was next to him. Bud Alden was kicking.

The Elmwood Rams were big, but they were clumsy. Something had set them off wrong—maybe it was Mimi's cheer, maybe it was just that they weren't on their own field—and they played badly. On the other hand, Woods Cross was in top form. Griswold's strategies worked, and somehow Griswold's machine worked too, smooth, without a flaw. Except for Bud.

Bud fumbled when he got the ball, losing it more than once to the Rams on first-down plays. Finally, by silent consent, the boys ignored Bud and didn't let him have the ball. Jim had it a few times and took it a couple of yards, but there was nothing spectacular about the first half. At halftime the score was 14–6, Woods Cross leading.

They headed for the locker room. Jim took a long swig from the fountain. Then he was aware someone was standing behind him. It was Bud.

"What was all that crap your girl friend spewed out?"

"Bad. Really bad," another boy put in. "Why does everyone act like Coach is dead?" Then the boy's face dropped. "He isn't, is he? I mean, they'd tell us, wouldn't they?"

"He isn't dead. Not by a long shot," Jim said. "He'll be back giving us hell in no time."

"He'd better be," Bud said, almost like a threat.

Jim smiled at his friend, realizing how few people had really gotten to the heart of what grief was all about. Dundee was right when he said there was a lot of anger involved.

The second half started poorly for the Rams. It had begun to rain, and the light mist that covered the field turned it into mud and made the ball slip out of their grasp. Griswold kept Bud out of the action and on the bench where he sat with a towel over his head, glowering at the field. Jim wondered if Bud would snap out of it and play well when Jake came back. Then he wondered if maybe he was fooling himself. Maybe Jake wasn't coming back.

The Rams made the kick, and Jim saw the ball coming his way. He reached up and took it from the air. He could hear the crowd break into a cheer. He started to run.

The ball, tucked neatly under his arm, became part of him. He headed for pay dirt. He'd been here be-fore—last night. Last night was just a rehearsal for what was happening now.

And the crowd was with him. "*Hal-bert, Hal-bert, Hal-bert,*" they shouted. He saw Mimi and the other girls leading the chant.

Then he remembered what his father had called

him—a Saturday hero. He faltered, looking around for a teammate. He caught a glimpse of yellow and brown just ahead of him. He swerved, but there was no blue and white anywhere. God, where are they? He had never felt so alone in all his life.

Somehow he cut through the Rams' defense and headed down the field. Then he saw Len just off to the side and another boy near him. He thought about making a lateral pass, but somehow the ball stayed tucked under his arm.

Len's hands were in the air, ready to receive, but as Jim passed him, he called, "Go for it, man!"

I'll be a Saturday hero, Jim told himself. I'll take the ball as far down the line as I can before they bring me down, or if they close in, I'll go out of bounds.

He saw the Rams closing in from the front door, but he lowered his head and charged toward them. Miraculously he slipped through. He could see the goalposts just ahead. He raised his head and called out to the air, to the crowd, to the boys in yellow and brown on either side of him and his own teammates wherever they were. Mostly he called to his dad waiting in the hospital. "This one's for Coach!"

"Jim Halbert carrying the ball, and he's over!" The voice blasted over the microphone.

And when Jim kicked the extra point, Woods Cross led by 21–6.

The Rams rallied after that, and the lead narrowed.

But after Jim's rush, the Woods Cross team put it together. They knew they could take the day, and they did, 27–20.

It was raining when they left the field, making it hard to distinguish one team from the other before the fracas was over. The autumn colors of brown and yellow were the same slate mud color as the blue and white.

As he passed the bench, his teammates' arms on his shoulders, Jim saw Mimi standing in the rain, her blond hair dark with wet and streaming down her back, her short skirt limp around her shapely thighs. Her blue eyes shone. She looked childlike standing there, and his heart went out to her. He went over.

"You were sensational," she said. "But then I knew you would be."

"I made one touchdown, Mimi. Len made two, and Bart Ramsay—"

"It was you who led it, saved the day. Did you hear me cheering for you?"

"I—I heard something."

She put her arms around him and hugged him, then drew back. She was covered with mud from his uniform. "*Yuck.* Look, I'll meet you at the car. I'll have to go home and change before we can go out. Where are we going?"

"The guys are going to Mandy's. I told them we'd be along later."

"Later? Why not now? I want to be part of the victory celebration. I want to be part of it all, Jim. I was a ninny to let so much time slip by. God, I almost lost you."

"I'll take you home to change and then pick you up later. I have something to do first."

She raised an eyebrow. "Something to do? What?" Then her eyes flashed. "Another date?"

In the streaming rain, with mud on her sweater and her face, Mimi lost her childlike appeal. She was still Mimi, still fussing about other girls, about other dates, about being part of everything as long as everything was on the winning side.

"Yes," he said, liking the way her face fell for a moment before she caught herself. "But I won't be long."

She turned. "Well, if that's the case, I'll get someone else to take me home. And to Mandy's." She started to leave.

As Jim knew she expected, he called her back. "Hey, Mimi, I'm sorry. I was just kidding. It isn't a date. Just something I have to do first." He put his arms around her.

The stands were empty, the streamers and pompoms lying forgotten on the bleachers, their colors running in the rain.

"What? What do you have to do?"

"See my dad. I want to tell him about the game.

The guys wanted to call him, but I told them I'd go see him."

"Well, why didn't you say so? Sure you want to do that. And I'd like to go with you. I want to be part of it, of all of it, Jim. The pain, too. I mean, I want to be there when you need me."

He didn't answer, he just looked at her. He felt she was moving away from him, or he from her. She was the Mimi who'd stood in front of the microphone making a mockery of his father's pain. "No, Mimi."

"No? Why not, Jim? I mean, you need somebody to be with you at a time like this. I've been a fool not to realize that before."

He thought about that. Yes, he did need somebody. And he was beginning to realize who that somebody was. "I want to go alone, Mimi." Then, seeing her disappointment, he added, "This time." That brought a smile.

"Did you like my cheer? The one I made up for him?"

"It was—uh—okay."

"Just okay? I worked like hell on that, Jim. I'm no poet, but I wanted to do something special, you know? I thought you'd like it."

"Did you do it for Dad? Or for me?"

"For your dad, of course. And for you, I guess. I mean, I'm sorry about screwing it up in the middle, but I covered it okay, don't you think?"

He sighed. "Yes, Mimi. You did. Look, let's get out of the rain. Here's the car key. Try not to get mud on the seat."

The guys had showered and were shouting and flipping each other with towels. When Jim entered, they let out a cheer.

Coach Griswold was standing off to one side, leaning against the door jamb of his office. "Hell of a run, Halbert. You dad would have been proud."

"No way," Jim said. "He'd have called me a Saturday hero."

"Yeah, and so you were. But there wasn't much you could do. We left a hole out there the size of the Grand Canyon. Nobody expected the interception." He clapped Jim on the shoulder. "Get showered. I've got to get out of here."

Griswold went into his office. Jim watched him standing at his desk, still wearing his rain-soaked sweats. He realized again how different it was for Griswold. Jake would have been out there with the boys, yelling at them, telling them what they did wrong. It didn't matter that they won. It mattered how they won, and Jake would have told them they played lousy. In some ways Jim missed that. It would be a while before they could accept this new way of being coached, being told they did well and then left alone to revel in it.

He turned, realizing what he had let into his mind.

It would take a while before they could accept this new way of being coached. Before they could accept Griswold. Suddenly he knew with certainty that he'd been fooling himself. Jake would not be back.

He did not join in the celebration, but dressed quickly and left. The others let him go as if they understood. Perhaps they did. Perhaps in the same moment the truth had struck Jim, it had struck them too.

20

Mimi was sitting quietly in the car. The mud had dried on her sweater. Her hair was limp, still wet. She looked bedraggled, like a drowned bird. He tossed her a towel, then got in beside her.

She toweled her hair and brushed at the dried mud. "What a night."

He didn't answer. He didn't feel much like making conversation, especially banalities about the weather. He wished he didn't have this date with her and wondered what it would cost him to break it. "Mimi, I'm not feeling too great tonight," he began.

"Sick?"

"No, just down."

"Down? How can you be down after that terrific—"

"About my dad. Sometimes I get down about him, you know?" He used it because it was a swift way to end any further questions. And because it was true.

"I'm sorry, Jim. I keep forgetting. I mean, I—"

"You keep forgetting. Like everyone else."

"I don't forget. I mean, God, who could forget about it? It's been so—so awful having him like he is. Sort of changing before your eyes. I remember how he used to roar down those halls, like a tank. Like a ship with all flags flying. Now he creeps like a mouse in and out of corners. Trying to look the same, but just not making it, you know? It's better now that he's in the hospital."

Jim stared at her for a long time. Finally he asked, "What's better about it?"

"What?"

"What's better about him being in the hospital?"

"Well, I mean, they can take care of him and everything."

"What you really mean is it's better for you, don't you?" Jim felt the sharp edge of his own words as they passed his lips.

"What? I don't know what you mean. Why should it be better for me?"

"You don't have to see him in the halls. You don't have to live with it day after day. He can be shut away from everyone, dying like a hero." Jim's anger rose as he spoke. A part of him realized it was not just Mimi he was condemning but himself as well, an earlier self who didn't want his father stalking the halls like a wounded beast.

"Jim, I—"

"You don't have to see him struggling with this monster called cancer. He can die there quietly, forgot—"

"Jim!" She said it sharply, like a slap on the face.

The anger went out of him, leaving him deflated. He leaned against the steering wheel, pressing his head against the cold plastic. "God, Mimi, it's hard."

"I know."

"I love the son of a bitch, you know that?"

"Sure you do." He felt her near him, her hand stroking his hair.

"But I didn't know it. It took this to make me realize it. God, Mimi, all those wasted years. Now, when it's too late, I realize what it was all about. He used to take me out on the lawn when I was practically still in diapers, you know? I never had a round ball like most kids—always a football. I think I was the most important thing that ever happened to him. Just about, anyway. A son, a chance to live it all over again. And I resented it all my life. Until now."

"You'll be as good as he was, Jim. You'll see."

He turned toward her. "No, Mimi. There's only one Jake Halbert."

"Look what you did today—that touchdown. Keep that up all season, and you'll be the star of Woods Cross. I'll be so proud of you."

"Mimi, have you heard anything I've been saying?"

"Of course I have. You've been talking about football. Come on, Jim, let's get going. I'm freezing to death, and I must look so awful. We can talk about it later."

Jim didn't say anything. He started the car and drove through the shining streets.

"What a rotten night," Mimi said. "I was hoping we could go to the Gulley. Make up for lost time, you know?" She giggled. "Come to think of it, it might be kind of fun. The rain beating on the roof of the car, everything private. What do you think?"

"I think the road will be streaming with mud, that's what I think," he said sourly.

"Oh, well, it was just a thought. There'll be other times." She cuddled up against him and put her damp head on his shoulder. "There'll be plenty of other times."

Jim thought about Gus. Why had she been so angry? He hadn't said all that much—just told her she reveled in being different. And suddenly she flew into a rage.

Then a memory that was tucked away in the file of his mind under "miscellaneous" drifted across his mind. He'd seen Len once when they were freshmen and his family had just moved to Woods Cross—his father starting his law practice. Len was smaller then, hovering between boyhood and manhood. Jim had caught a glimpse of him in an alcove of the building, flat against the brick wall, his eyes wide with terror. Two boys, seniors by the look of them, were facing him, their hands clenched into fists.

Jim hadn't stopped, hadn't taken in the significance of what he'd seen, merely glanced and walked away. Now the memory came back and he understood.

So who was he to tell Gus or Len or anybody that they don't try to fit in? When he himself fit in like the last piece of a jigsaw puzzle. There was a place for him at Woods Cross, always had been. What did he know about it, anyway?

Suddenly he wanted to see her, be with her, hear her thin laugh and hold her in his arms. He didn't want to be with Mimi. He wanted to be with Gus.

He pulled up to Mimi's house. "Look, I'll wait while you change. And then I'll take you to Mandy's."

"Great. I was hoping you'd say that and forget all this silliness about going to the hospital. I mean, I think you should go and everything, but if we went now, we'd miss all the fun the guys are having. I mean, you can tell your dad all about the game later, can't you?"

"I—I suppose I could."

She squeezed his hand. "I won't be a minute."

He leaned back against the seat and watched the rain stream down the windshield. He tried to empty his mind of all thoughts.

Mimi came back, wearing a powder blue skirt and sweater with a see-through raincoat over them. Her hair, blow-dried and shining, seemed to float around her head like a halo. She was beautiful.

"See? That didn't take long. Boy, was I a mess. No wonder you were such a grump." She leaned over and kissed his cheek, putting her arms around his neck and bringing her face close to his. "Too bad about the Gulley," she whispered, " 'cause I really want you to-night, hero."

He had turned toward her, feeling the rise of desire. But the word stopped him cold. He put his hands on her shoulders and drew her away. "Let's go."

"Now what's wrong?"

"You wanted to go to Mandy's. Let's go to Mandy's."

"So you're still a grump."

"Yes." They drove in silence through the wet streets. At Mandy's he pulled up to the curb.

"You'd better not park here," she told him. "You'll get a ticket. Why not go around the back?"

"I'm not coming in."

"What? Not coming in?"

"No. I'm going to the hospital. Like I said."

"You're going to dump me here? Like some creep who couldn't get a date?"

"You wanted to be part of the celebration. So go in and be part of it. I'm going to see my dad."

She wavered between reaching out to him and getting out of the car. "Will you be back?"

"I don't know. I'm not sure. One of the guys'll take you home if I'm not."

"That's not what's worrying me, Jim. I—" She paused and looked out at the rain, then spoke. "What went wrong, Jim?"

"What?"

"I thought we could make it—get back together. But we can't, can we?"

"No, Mimi, I don't think so."

"Was it something I said? Was it because of Milo?"

"Milo? Oh, no, nothing like that."

"Because if it was, I've forgotten all about him. It's really over now."

"No, Mimi, it isn't because of Milo."

"Then tell me!" She became petulant, like a child stamping her foot. "What can I do? How can I change? I want you, Jim. I want to be part of everything you are and everything you're going to be. I don't want to be left out."

He waited a long time before he answered. He even considered not answering at all. "Mimi, you won't be left out. Go on into Mandy's and be part of the victory celebration."

"You'll come along later?"

"I don't know. I don't think so. Get one of the guys to take you home."

"Will you call me tomorrow, then?"

"No, Mimi."

She studied him, her clear blue eyes shining with tears. Then she flipped her head, the blond hair flashing like the mane of a beautiful horse. "Okay, if that's the way you want it." She got out of the car and ran into Mandy's.

Jim drove to the cheese shop. He got out and went down the alley where he'd seen Gus disappear the first night when he'd driven her home. There was a rickety stairway leading up to a door on the side of the building.

The door had once been green, but the color had turned in the weather to a sickly gray-green, like a threatening sky. He found no doorbell, so he rapped sharply on the door. Immediately a dog began to bark, then a baby started to cry, and finally a man swore.

The door opened, and the sharp nose of a black mongrel protruded. Above it, but not very far, the solemn face of a skinny girl studied him suspiciously. She looked like a smaller version of Gus, only with a softer face, more vulnerable. Without Gus's mask, he realized. He wanted to take the child into his arms and soothe it, protect it from the world that made Gus so hard. Instead he asked for Gus.

"She ain't here." The girl removed a finger from

her mouth long enough to answer, then replaced it.

The door opened farther and the dog came out, sniffing around Jim's ankles and plunging its nose between his legs. Absently Jim scratched its head.

A man had come to the door and stood over the child. "What d'you want?"

Again Jim saw a version of Gus—this time the mask of defensiveness strongly in place. But the vulnerability peered out of his eyes like a frightened animal in a lair.

"I—I wanted to see Gus. I'm a friend of hers," Jim said.

"She's at work. Got a job down at that there restaurant."

"Restaurant?"

"On the corner, up the street. Working instead of wasting her time with school. Only it ain't much of a job," he added.

Jim realized he meant Mandy's. Under any other circumstances he would have laughed at Mandy's being called a restaurant. But there was no humor in this man, or in the way he spat out the word "school."

"Sorry to bother you. Uh, do you know when she'll be finished?"

"Later. Around seven." He started to close the door.

For a moment Jim wanted to push it forward and confront the man, Gus's father. Jim was easily a head taller than the man and much stronger. He had the insane urge to beat his head in until he listened to reason. Gus must not quit school, be reduced to this kind of life—waiting tables, then getting married and ending up like this. Not Gus. She deserved better.

"Trip, get in here," Gus's father called to the dog, but before the sentence was out, he began to cough—a deep, liquid cough. He closed the door on Jim, on the world outside that had dealt with him so cruelly. He wouldn't have understood even if Jim beat him to a pulp. It was Gus Jim needed to reach.

He couldn't go to Mandy's to look for her, not with Mimi there. He drove on to the hospital.

His mother had not yet come. His father's room was dark, and the rain pelted against the windows. His father lay on his back, snoring. Jim crept up to the bed and stood looking down. Asleep Jake looked vulnerable.

Jake's eyelids fluttered. "What? Jim, is that you, boy?"

"Yes, Dad. I didn't mean to wake you up."

Jake slid up. "Hell, all I do in this place is sleep. How was the game?"

"We won. 27–20."

"27–20? What's the matter? Couldn't you make it any tighter?"

"We tried, Dad. But they just wouldn't let us."

"The Rams were always the best. They'll probably take State this year."

"Hell they will! We'll take State. Like always."

Jake leaned back against the pillows and smiled. "You're not a strong team this year, Jim. And Griswold hasn't the knack to get the best out of you. It'll take more time than he's got to turn you clowns into a team."

"Griswold? What are you talking about? You're the coach. You'll take us to State."

Jake didn't answer for a long time, just smiled to himself as if enjoying a private joke. Finally he said, "Can't, Jim. Don't want to."

"Don't want to? Dad?"

"Your mother wants some time with me. I've got a few months at most. Maybe we can do some traveling."

"But, Dad—"

"I've given a lot to that team, Jim, to those boys."

"I know, Dad—"

"Maybe it's time to let go. They've been giving me this drug—penta something. Same stuff they give to criminals to get them to talk. Truth serum. Ever had it?"

"No, Dad."

"Hell of a trip. Makes you feel all cozy. Maybe they call it truth serum because it helps you see the truth. Knocks down your defenses." He chuckled. "And old Jake has a lot of defenses. Must be good stuff." He closed his eyes and seemed to drift off, then

opened them again. "I won't go right away, of course.
Give Griswold a hand. He's too easy on you. Acts like
he likes you. Got to teach him to hate you—and to get
you guys to hate him. That's the way. Who scored the
winning touchdown?"

"Hard to say. We led all the way."

"You do anything? Or just sit on your butt?"

"I—I ran one."

"What yardage?"

"Uh—seventy-five. About."

"Seventy-five yards? You took the ball seventy-
five yards?"

"Yeah, I know. Saturday hero again. But there
wasn't anybody—"

"That's your strength, Jim, same as it was mine.
Rushing. You should concentrate on that. Don't try to
pass, you're no good at it. Once you get the ball, hang
on to it and take it in."

"But, Dad—"

"What about Wilson?"

"Steady. As always."

"Alden?"

"Benched again. Second half."

"Jesus Christ, doesn't Griswold know anything?
You can't bench Alden during a scrimmage. On the
bench he's like a bad conscience. You see him there,
and you play lousy. I can see I've got a lot to get across
to Griswold."

Just then a nurse came into the room. "Almost dinner time, Mr. Halbert." She beamed. "I've got to get you washed up. Oh, hello." She turned the beam on Jim.

"Can't it wait? My son here just won a game. Took the ball seventy-five yards for a t.d."

The nurse's expression didn't change. "How nice. I guess I can do the other rooms first. I'll be back."

"Your mother tell you? They say I can go home tomorrow."

"Dad, that's great."

"I won't be much good, though. Got to get my strength back." He lay against the pillows, his eyes dark in the half light of the room. "Jim, I want you to promise me something."

"Sure, Dad."

"I hate this place—all starch and soft voices. I don't want to die here. Not here." He closed his eyes and took a deep breath. "When my time comes, boy, I want to finish up at home. Promise me you won't let them take me here again."

His hand, groping, caught Jim's wrist.

Jim wanted to say, I'll tell Mom, or, Isn't it up to Mom? or something like that—to shift the responsibility on to someone else. But he was remembering the run on the field, and the cheers. Those cheers formed a bond between father and son that would never be broken.

"All right, Dad. I promise."

Jake let go and settled back on his pillow. "Hell of a business," he said. "Took care of myself all my life. Didn't smoke, didn't booze, exercised. And here I am. Weak as a kitten. Taken care of by women. Hell of a deal." Suddenly he caught his breath. His face contorted with pain. He held his side, knotting the sheets up in his fists. His eyes disappeared into the deep wrinkles on his face. Then he let out his breath in a long sigh and relaxed.

Jim's eyes stung with tears. He reached out, touched the air between them, afraid to touch his father, but wanting to. "Dad—"

Jake wouldn't meet his eye. "What they put in that hospital food, I have no idea. It gives me the worst damned gas pains."

More lies, Jim thought. Just when his father had started to open up, to talk about his dying. Jim knew he didn't want to let it pass, whatever it cost him.

He touched his father. "Dad, how long has it been like this? How long have you had pain like this?"

"Pain? Hell, that's just a touch of indigestion. Like I said, the hospital food—"

"It's pain, Dad. And you've had it a long time."

Jakes eyes searched the room, then finally met Jim's. "Don't tell your mother," he said.

His mother was at his side every night here in the hospital and before that at home with him all night.

How could she not know? "Dad, take it easy. Don't fight it. It's okay."

"Hell of a deal," Jake said again, leaning back. The sweat stood out on his forehead, gleaming in the light from the bedside table. "I've got to get out of here— get back on the field. Griswold can't carry the ball this year. And this year it matters."

"It's always mattered, Dad. Every year."

"Yeah, that's true. Hell. I've got eleven trophies down there in that game room. But I want an even dozen."

"We'll do our best, Dad."

"Alden. What's the matter with the kid? I give him a place on the team, even though he's a midget, and he lets me down."

"I've often wondered why you did that, Dad. Gave Bud a spot."

"Believe me, so have I." He looked at Jim, realizing he was really asking. "Christ, because I'm a softy, that's why. Maybe I remember how he used to work out with us, I don't know. Maybe I thought I owed him. Never do that again." He closed his eyes.

Jim saw him grimace, and his hands under the blanket clutched once more at his side. Then he was still. Jim thought he had fallen asleep, but just as he was about to get up, his father opened his eyes.

"You never liked it much, did you?" His voice was a whisper.

"What, Dad?"

"The game. You never took to it."

"Not like you did, Dad. I guess I never realized what the cheers of the crowd can do for you. The love they give."

"Yeah. That's what it's all about. Taking the ball in all the way. Hell, that's a good feeling. I wanted you to know that feeling, Jim. That's all I ever wanted."

He squeezed his father's hand. "I do know it, Dad. I've felt it."

"You have? Today when you took the ball in?"

"Yes. And earlier." Last night, he thought. Running alone on the soggy turf and hearing the wind cheer like a crowd.

"You take an awful chance, you know, rushing like that," Jake said. "You could fumble or be brought down. If you think they're going to catch you, go out of bounds. That way you don't lose the ball."

"I'll remember that, Dad."

"But if you think you can take it, take it in, boy. All the way."

Jim cleared a lump out of his throat. A question hung in the air between them. "Dad, I did that once, remember? Ran it in for ninety-five yards."

Jake opened his eyes wider. "Yeah, that's right. I'd forgotten."

Forgotten? Jim thought. He'd thought of little else but that day when he was on the field, and his father had forgotten about it. "You benched me. Called me a Saturday hero."

"Yeah, I guess I did. You took a hell of a chance. Might have blown the whole game."

"But, you just said if I think I can take it in—"

"You got to learn balance, boy. It's one thing to take the ball seventy-five yards when you've got a clear track. It's another to play Saturday hero and run it in just to show off."

"How do you know I wasn't showing off today?"

"I don't. Were you?"

"I don't know. I—I remembered what you said, and I looked around. I didn't see any of the guys."

"That's the difference. You did what you had to. That's what makes the difference between a real player and a Saturday hero. A real player does what he has to. He doesn't do it to make a splash in the news. He does it because he's playing for a team and wants to win for that team. You follow me?"

Jim nodded. "Yes, Dad, I think so."

"I guess I was pretty hard on you that day, boy. I think it was because of something else. Something I've never told anyone before, not even your mother."

"What, Dad?"

"You know why I left Miami after only one season?"

"No, Dad. Mom said it's because she didn't like the life—traveling all over, hardly ever home."

"Nah, that's not the real reason. She thinks I did it for her—left the pros—but that's not true. It's what I told her, but the fact of the matter is, I washed out."

"You, Dad? I can't believe it. You were the best."

"I was a Saturday hero, boy. I didn't know how to work with a team. I played like I owned the field. I was good all right, and it got me through college. But when I got with real players, seasoned players, I was a washout. So when I saw you on the field that day doing the same goddamned thing, I took you apart. And I'll do it again too. You can count on it."

He pulled his hand out of Jim's and brought the blanket up to his chin. "By the way, boy, that's just between you and me. Don't let on to your mother or anybody."

"No, Dad." He helped his father smooth the bed clothes, then gently brought his lips to his father's forehead. "Thanks, Dad."

When the nurse came back to serve her patient dinner, he was asleep, his hand in Jim's.

21

Jim waited in his car down the street from Mandy's until he saw Mimi come out. Seeing her in her plastic raincoat, her long blond hair catching the light as she passed under the street lamp, he wanted to call to her. He wished he could make it all the way it was, but he knew that wasn't possible. Things would never be the same.

She turned, and he realized she was not alone. A boy from the team—Gary, someone whom he knew only slightly—was walking with her. Mimi didn't waste any time grieving over lost loves, he thought.

After they'd turned the corner, Jim got out of his car and went up the street to Mandy's. The small room was nearly empty. Mandy was behind the counter as usual, wiping it with a cloth, but Jim noticed the cloth and the counter were clean. Bud and Len were sitting in one of the booths, and Gus was leaning against their table, laughing with them. She was wearing a large white apron over her jeans. At Jim's entrance, she turned and scowled.

"Hey, man, you made it. We were about to close up here and give up on you," Len called. "How's your dad?"

"Giving them hell at the hospital. Ready to come home."

Gus started back toward the counter, but Jim stopped her. "Stay, Gussie," he said, calling her by an affectionate name he'd heard one of her brothers use that first night when he'd called her.

She stopped, but she wouldn't meet his eye. "Got to finish up. We close in ten minutes."

"I came to take you out to dinner."

She looked up, and he saw in her eyes the same vulnerability he'd seen in the eyes of her father. Some of her guard was down, she was open to being hurt again.

"Where?" she asked.

"Any place you'd like. Except the Gaslight, of course."

"The Gaslight? What's the Gaslight?"

"Most expensive restaurant in town. French."

"*Humm.* I always did like it French." Then she tossed her head. "Wouldn't fit in there, though, would I?"

"Gus, you'd fit in anywhere. And you know it."

She smiled and went toward the counter, the

glasses on the tray she was carrying chinking. He slid in next to Bud.

"What'd your dad think about the game?" Len asked.

"Asked if we couldn't have made a bigger score. I think he was pleased."

"When's he coming back?" Bud asked.

"Tomorrow."

"I mean to school. When's he coming back to coach?"

Better get it said, Jim thought. "He isn't."

"What?"

"He wants to travel. Spend some time with Mom. He isn't coming back to school."

"He can't do that. Not right now. The middle of the season."

"It's not exactly the middle. One game. And he didn't coach that one."

"He can't do that to us. We've got to take State. My last year. After that it doesn't matter, but this year—"

"Bud, shut up!" Len's voice was sharp like a shot.

Bud's head flipped up.

"Just shut up," Len repeated. "Listen to yourself. Whining because Coach isn't going to coach the team. I sat here tonight listening to you guys until I thought I'd puke. Coach is dying. He's got just a few months. And you're worrying about the team, for Christ's sake." He looked over at Jim. "Sorry, man. But it's got to be said."

Jim nodded.

"But Griswold is a creep. We'll never take State with Griswold," Bud persisted.

"So we don't take State. Big deal. We'll play the best we can, and whether it's Griswold or the man in the moon, we'll be playing for Coach. We've got that at least. The guys that come after us will hear about him—probably for years to come. But we will be the last senior class to have known him. Think about that one."

Jim put his hand on Bud's shoulder. "He'll come in and work with Griswold. He told me that."

"Griswold hates me. Won't put me in the game."

"Bud, he will in time. And Dad told me he'd talk to Griswold about that, too."

Bud's eyes sought his. "Yeah? He did?"

"Yes. He said it was a mistake to keep you out."

Bud grinned. "You wouldn't be bullshitting me, would you?"

"No. He really said that. As soon as he gets back. But you've got to deserve it, Bud. Dad doesn't do any favors, you know."

"Man, do I ever know that."

"Come on, guys, we'd better clear out of this place. I think they want to close." Len slid out of the booth, then called across the room. "Gus, baby, a million thanks. You give the place class."

"Go on," she said, but she was smiling.

"I mean it, girl. Now, you think over what I said, hear?"

Jim waited while Gus finished up.

The streets shone under the lights and the air smelled clean. "I love it when it's been raining," she said.

"What was all that with you and Len? What were you supposed to think over?"

Gus looked up at him, her face impish. "Now, wouldn't you just like to know?"

"Okay, so don't tell me."

She took his arm. "He told me not to quit school. Said he almost did when he first came, it was so rough. But he didn't."

"He's right, you know, I told you—"

"Don't start with me again. I'm letting you back into my life with a lot of misgivings. I don't want any lectures—not from you. From Len it's different, because he knows what he's talking about. He's been on the outside too. You haven't. So you really don't know what it's like."

"What makes you think I don't?"

"Hell, look at you. Woods Cross written all over you. You've been part of the crowd since there was a crowd, right?"

"Yes, I guess that's true. But I do know what it's like, Gus. I didn't before, but I do now. I was ready to quit this year on the first day back."

"Hell you were."

"I felt like a leper. Everybody treating me different. Because of my dad. But now I'm glad I stuck it out."

Gus gave his arm a squeeze. "There I go again. Every time I make a positive statement, I'm wrong. I didn't even think about that. Hell, I sure know what that one's like. But I won't get started on my own dad again." They'd reached the car. "Should I go home and change? I do own another outfit, believe it or not. In fact, if I dug deep enough, I might find a dress."

"No, you're fine. Unless you want to change, that is."

"Another time, then. I'd like to dress up for you, show you I'm not so bad-looking. I'm not dressed right for that there Frenchy place, but I guess I'll do for Burger King."

She devoured three hamburgers and then leaned back. "I haven't eaten all day. Sorry."

"I'm glad I didn't take you to the Gaslight."

"Yeah. But you owe me that one. And I collect my debts."

He liked the permanence of that statement.

"Guess what Mandy's going to let me do?" She went on. "You know how dull those walls are, how bad they need painting?"

"You're going to paint the place?"

"Yep."

"Gus, you're kidding. He's taking advantage of you."

"Maybe. But I'm not going to just paint them. I'm going to do a mural. I've got to work out what it's going to be, but I've got some ideas."

"A mural? You mean paint pictures on the wall?"

"Yeah. I got the idea that first night I went there. We were sitting in the booth and I was facing that wall, the one behind the counter. And you gave me back that paper where I'd scribbled the kids in math. I think it would be fun to do faces—the faces of the kids who hang out in Mandy's. Maybe some of the teachers too. Or the team. What do you think?"

Jim transferred the faces she'd drawn on the yellow paper to the wall in Mandy's. "That's a great idea, Gus."

"Len Wilson said so."

"Len Wilson again, huh?"

Gus blushed. He'd never seen her do that before, it was becoming. "Hell, Jim, we're just friends. But anyway, Len had an idea about the mural. He thinks I ought to put your dad in it. What do you think? Do you think he'd mind?"

"Mind? He'd be crazy about the idea."

"I'd have to do some sketches, though. I don't remember what he looks like."

"Drop by. He'll be home this weekend."

"You sure? I mean, he's been in the hospital.

Maybe he needs some time to relax. Get used to being home."

"He'll be up the wall by Sunday. It'd be a good way to keep him quiet. Besides, I'd like you to meet him."

"I already did. I have him for gym, remember? Had, that is." Suddenly she looked sad.

"Gus, you should go back."

"Look, Jim, I thought about it. After what you said this morning about not trying to fit in, I thought about it hard. I can be pig-headed, I know that. But this time it ain't Gus that's out of step. It's the system. I can't operate in a place like that—a pass for this, a pass for that. Hell, you need a pass to piss in that joint."

"And you're going to let it beat you? The system?"

"I can't see any other way."

He studied her face for a long time, liking it, wishing he didn't have to say what he was about to. "Gus Palmer, I didn't figure you for a quitter."

Her head shot up. "We Palmers—"

"You're quitting, Gus. You're giving up in the first round. You've been at Woods Cross exactly two weeks—not even that—and you're quitting. Why? Because it got a little rough, that's why."

"Jim, I know what you're saying, and I've thought about that, too. But I can't make it there. Like the song says, I gotta be free."

"Free? What kind of free is that? One school, a couple of tight-assed teachers and a few snobby kids, and you're out. So you're going to work in a place like Mandy's the rest of your life just because somebody didn't look at you the right way."

"I won't stay there. I'll finish school somehow." Jim wished he didn't have to look at her face. She looked so miserable.

"How?"

"Night school or something. I don't want to end up like Mom with a mess of kids and no money. I know that."

"And us? What about us?"

"What about us?"

"You think I want to go out with a girl who quit school? Who works as a *waitress*?" He said it as if it were the worst possible job.

"There's no shame in waitin' tables," Gus retorted.

"Not if it's to pick up some extra cash—to go to college or something."

"College? Me go to college? You're puttin' me on."

"You could, Gus. You could do anything you wanted."

She smiled. "Sometimes I think you're right. But then I say to myself, 'Gus, baby, you're out of your league. Way out.' Gus Palmer in college! That's a laugh."

"Wouldn't you like to, Gus?"

"No. But I'd kind of like to—hell, you'll laugh if I tell you."

"No, I won't."

"I'd kind of like to go somewhere and study art. I mean that's the main reason I want to do the mural. To get some practice."

"Then you'd better go back to school and finish."

"I'll think about it, okay? Now, lay off."

He drove her home, pulling into the same place in front of the cheese shop. He knew he'd be seeing a lot of that cheese shop in the months to come.

A few people passed, going to the movies or to Baskin-Robbins for ice cream. Jim drew Gus's face close and kissed her.

She responded, then pulled away. "I'm really out of my league," she said again. "Take it slow, Jim. Give me a chance to get used to it."

She got out of the car, then leaned down and spoke to him through the open window. "I'll give it some thought, Jim—going back to school. Waitin' tables is hard work. And maybe it won't be so bad being there—at school, I mean. Anyway, I'll drop by your place on Sunday and see your dad. If you're sure he won't mind."

"I'll pick you up about twelve."

As he drove home, Jim thought about his father, the way he was holding out on everyone, not admitting his pain or his weakness.

But then Jim remembered a game they'd played when he was a sophomore. It had been touch and go all the way, right up to the last few minutes. They were so close to paydirt they could taste it, but they couldn't seem to break through. Then the clock ran out.

The guys had gone back to the locker room dejected, but Jake had bawled them out. "Look, you lummoxes, don't ever say you lost. You didn't lose. The damned clock ran out, that's all."

Jim smiled to himself. Jake wasn't holding out on anyone, he was holding on, the way he always did, trying to make that winning score before the clock ran out.

BARBARA STRETTON grew up in Salt Lake City, graduated from the University of Utah and holds a Masters of Library Science from Southern Connecticut State College. She has taught junior and senior high school English, has been a school librarian, and currently writes scripts for educational filmstrips, teaches business communications and runs a writers workshop. Other interests include playing the violin, sculpting and marathon running. She lives with her husband in Old Greenwich, Connecticut. *You Never Lose* is her second novel.